D1569466

Acclaim for
Cardinal and Other Stories

"I love the mind at work in these wonderfully strange stories about so-called ordinary life. They go right to the heart of how uncanny, even bizarre, ordinary life really is, if you're paying attention. This is not 'absurdist' work. It's ultra-realism. It's evidence of a new, fresh voice—intelligent, strange, deeply familiar, oddly funny, pleasantly disturbing. Add Higley's stories to my favorites."
- Brad Watson, author of *Aliens in the Prime of Their Lives* and *Miss Jane: A Novel*

"Alex Higley has a poet's eye that registers the light and the dark with equal insight, an eye that sees the welter and wiles of humanity with precision, pathos, and humor. In these twenty stories, Higley memorably explores questions related to love, friendship, mortality, the powerful grip of the past, regret, desire. A very impressive debut."
- Christine Sneed, author of *Portraits of a Few of the People I've Made Cry* and *Little Known Facts*

"Few books have captivated me like Alex Higley's collection of deft and compact stories. Even fewer contain such a variety of compelling characters—from erudite security guards, to clandestine ufologists, to a little boy who insists

on reminding his second grade class that they're going to die. Unlike so much of what I read now, the brilliance of Higley's stories is subtle and implicit, utterly at the service of the heartbreaking truths about which they're built. *Cardinal* is a remarkable debut, and Alex Higley is a writer with a career to watch."
- Naeem Murr, author of *The Perfect Man*

"'It's late morning, Sunday, bright and green October,' is how the scene is set at the opening of 'Cardinal,' the title story in Alex Higley's compelling collection. Higley is a writer whose gift for capturing the daylight lit surface of ordinary life is a cover for the undercurrents and shadows his fiction explores. Higley's collection with its quick-paced, page-turning narratives and its clear, artful writing is anything but ordinary."
- Stuart Dybek, author of *The Coast of Chicago: Stories* and *I Sailed with Magellan*

"One of my favorite discoveries in the past year is the writer Alex Higley. His stories develop so cleanly and powerfully that it's hard to believe this is his first book. Admirers of Frederick Barthelme and Brad Watson—you now have a new writer to cherish."
- Shane Jones, author of *Daniel Fights a Hurricane* and *Crystal Eaters*

Cardinal

and Other Stories

Alex Higley

TP

TAILWINDS PRESS

Copyright © 2017 by Alex Higley. All rights reserved. Except as permitted under the U.S. Copyright Act of 1976, no part of this publication may be reproduced, distributed, or transmitted in any form or by any means, or stored in a database or retrieval system, without the written permission of the publisher.

An excerpt from the website of the Mathematisches Forschungsinstitut Oberwolfach (www.mfo.de) appears in "Wolf is a River in Germany." Excerpts from the Wikipedia entry on "Phoenix Lights" (en.wikipedia.org/wiki/Phoenix_Lights) appear, in modified form, in "Rhymes with Feral." An excerpt from the Al-Jazeera article, "Lax gun laws in Indiana fuel gun violence in Chicago" (america.aljazeera.com/articles/2016/1/11/lax-gun-laws-in-indiana-fuel-violence-in-chicago.html), appears in "How I Got This Job."

Tailwinds Press
P.O. Box 2283, Radio City Station
New York, NY 10101-2283
www.tailwindspress.com

Published in the United States of America
ISBN: 978-0-9967175-2-6
1st ed. 2017

Contents

For Brittany

Cardinal

Surfers

We are buying groceries in bustling mid-winter Phoenix following Ann's doctor's appointment. This was a follow-up appointment, and things are progressing as the doctor expected. We didn't know what to expect, so his expectations have become our own. Ann will wear the eye patch for another week. The snowbirds are back, the streets and aisles made dangerous by their comic inattention, their not so secret hopes for death, for taking others with them. That's one of Ann's big theories, that so many people "act like they'd rather be dead." She makes a distinction between "acting" like one wants to be dead, and actually wanting to be dead. She means "acting" as in taking action and as in performing. And she also separates all this from wanting "to die." She says, "No one wants *to die* but plenty of people act like they want to *be dead*." I don't know what I think about this. I've heard it all many times. Movies with Ann are fun, clearly.

My wife is pushing our cart slowly, her left eye behind a black patch. A middle aged blonde woman in a light sweater and black eye patch gets stares. Bent over in front of two types of coconut sugar an old woman is saying, "Nogales, Nogales, Nogales," and her husband completes the quavering thought standing behind her as he blocks all passage, "Mexico. Where we were is not a place we can any longer be. New Mexico. Grab three sugar bags. New sugar bags."

Everywhere in this city old people are speaking aloud terrifying half-omens and falsehoods. Often these very people are carrying guns. The term is "open carry," which my wife cites as proof of her pet theory. She said the quickness of the gun is related to wanting to be dead, but not wanting to die, this desire. This is evidence I believe in, even if the conclusion strikes me as somewhat morbid. I can tell you old people speaking aloud to shelved sugar does not get stares. Just the opposite.

No one in the store has asked about my wife's patch yet, "What happened?" or "Didn't have that last time you were in, did you?" But the threat that someone might ask has her anxious, so we walk slowly meting out our steps just so, as if because we keep moving no one will be able to successfully speak to us.

Ann's embarrassed by the procedure she's had, embarrassed because of what her condition is commonly referred to, "surfer's eye." She's a woman from the Bronx, a private woman, a woman who reluctantly married me, reluctantly lives in the west, but in most other situations acts with certainty and absolute belief. She's not often sick or hobbled, and for this reason, I feel the patch is particularly fucking with her. That, and the fact that when she called her sister in Connecticut to explain the procedure her sister already knew all about the condition, and interrupted Ann to say, "Yes, the surfer thing. Will you have to cancel the trip?"

In the grocery store my wife says, "I hate that we came in here. Can we—"

I tell her, "Of course," and we leave the cart where it is behind the sugar man, an act I hate to witness from others, the abandonment of carts, but an act I make to show my wife she is more important than me not being understood as an asshole to the immediate public. She leads the way out of the store and its familiar songs, lighting, attitudes, and stands at the edge of the parking lot as if the ocean is in front of her, waves crashing. She turns to me, and when I see the look on her face, I jog to catch up.

The trip her sister referred to is for our niece's high school graduation. We are told the party will be muted because college is not on the horizon, or a job, but instead a move-in with a boyfriend in the city, a musician. The couple has expressed long-term plans to land in California.

The family is mostly aghast because he has a tattoo on his face. A small arrow, point down, next to his right eye. No one has asked him the significance, which shocked me, because it was the first thing I wanted to know when my wife relayed all this pre-trip information to me. Vital family gossip. Instead of having an answer to my question, she told me what she was told following the tattoo reveal, "He's a Native American. But Laura doesn't know whether to call him Native American or indigenous."

"Why would she call him indigenous?" I ask. We are home, slowly drinking wine. We are across the living room from one another, my wife watching TV with the closed captioning on from the couch and I'm lying on the floor. She mutes the TV when she thinks she can hear the neighbors beginning to yell at each other, but it has been quiet for a while now and she's left the sound off.

"Columbus Day has her all fucked up. Indigenous Peoples' Day, you know?"

"Oh, right. If we are just talking about words, I like the sound of American Indian," I say.

"We aren't just talking about words," Ann says, "The whole point is we aren't talking about words, we are talking about a man, the boyfriend."

"Well why would she have to say any of these words in front of him?"

"She doesn't. She just wants to get it right."

"She wants to get it right in her head. She wants to get right, in her head."

I tell my wife it sounds like maybe her sister should move in with face tattoo, so she'd have time to figure out what to call him. This does not go over so well. But I do think my stance/ignorance/indifference has helped unite Ann with Laura, at least in Ann's thinking, and this will benefit me once we actually get out to clean, wooded Connecticut.

From across the room, the tattoo is not noticeable, and seeing this young man in a cable-knit sweater and khakis, the word "indigenous" feels of the wrong language. I think, isn't that a plant word? Coniferous? His black hair is short and parted, and it's clear that he had parents who paid for braces. The town we are in is called Hamden. I like being sent out on errands, there have been two such occasions this afternoon since we got back from the ceremony, and I have decided to not start drinking until later in the day so I can continue these runs. Both trips have been to the grocery store, and each time I have had the overwhelming desire to stop a man a generation older than myself, in front of the rye bread, and tell him where I live armed men can walk in and purchase a quart of skim milk without any trouble. That a woman with a gun and two children holster high can buy paper towels and is given free rein. And yet an old woman with a blind Westie shaking in her cart is asked to leave. Someone might be allergic. I have wanted to tell these men, grayer than me, about this place, Arizona, but I can't imagine they'd believe me in the way I'd want them to, for them to understand this is not just common or notable but the constant reality. It's not TV news, it's real life. And they'd maybe ask, well, why do you live there? And I'd have no answer. Maybe Canada would come up if we talked long enough, or Norway or Japan. Other essentially gunless places. Maybe if we found a bar I'd tell them, uncertain if it was true, that maybe I live where I do because I'd rather be dead. But this wouldn't be true. The worst it gets for me is the incomplete sentence, "Reasons to not kill myself," getting stuck in my head. But the reasons never come. There is no need to generate any argument to live, because I don't get beyond having the line "Reasons to not kill myself," repeating in my thoughts. In this hypothetical bar, I'd be glad Ann wasn't with me to join in their questioning.

I return to the bright house with the champagne and as I come in the door I am face to face with face tattoo, who I have not formally been introduced to yet. The house is crowded with family, all my wife's sisters, and the ghostly living grandparents, rabbit-like grandchildren, the house is loud, and so it's normal we haven't shaken hands yet. He tells me his name is Chris, and repeats my name back to me after I say it, and I can't help myself, I say,

"Indigenous is what the sisters were speculating might be the right word for you."

"That sounds like a very Connecticut conclusion," he says.

"Not necessarily bad—"

"Yeah, not necessarily anything," Chris says.

I resist asking him where he is from, but I feel now that he is from Connecticut. Later I want to Google what percentage of the Connecticut population is Native American. I ask, "What type of music do you play?"

He says, "Why does everyone keep asking me that?"

I'm confused. I say, "I thought you were a musician?"

He says, "I had a band for while. But, I'm a student. I'm in graduate school for Dream Studies."

Initially when he said "student" I was going to tell him that the reason everyone is calling him a musician is because then the "musician with a tattoo on his face" formulation could be used. Not that this is a widely accepted cliché, but it does seem to broadcast a certain type of joblessness and doom. But now that he's said "Dream Studies" in a way that lets me know both those words are to be capitalized, it seems the most damning relevant caricature was not painted.

"What school?" I ask, striving to project innocence, earnestness, eagerness for the answer.

"Saybrook University. I'm in their online Dream Studies graduate certificate program, year two."

"Of?"

"Year two of two."

I remember working with a woman who one day went around to everyone in the office, and when she got someone alone near the fax machine or the coffee, explained calmly that the world was flat. It was incredible to experience. In my case, she said she "had news" for me and then, rarely blinking, told me her story. At first, I thought I was the only one who she was revealing her findings to, but, over time we all found each other and amazedly understood she'd been telling *everyone* we worked with that the world was flat. This was around 2005 or 2006. She said that NASA had faked all of their photos of our planet, depicted Earth as falsely round, as had other countries, and that we were all being duped. I had nodded throughout her explanation and maybe said, "Interesting," and others had done some version of the same, but one man I worked with, an older guy, had said, "Why do other planets look round when I look in my telescope?" She couldn't answer that, but said she'd find out. This was early in my marriage, when we were new to Arizona, and no doubt colored my feelings about the state. Anyway this is what I'm thinking about as Chris is telling me about his Dream Studies program. I feel like he is about to say something that will separate himself from me entirely, or at least even further than the fact that he is in a Dream Studies program.

I tell him I am skeptical of such a program, not that the area of study is not worthy, it is, but that it seems like the kind of scam program that would proliferate in California.

Chris says, "That's fair. But maybe I want to be a person that participates in scam culture. Maybe I want to set up shop in one of these beach towns with bored rich folks willing to pay to have their dreams deconstructed and offered back up as motivation." I don't tell him this but I believe having a tattoo on his face and not being white will help him in this venture.

I take a small step back from Chris without realizing I am doing so, but when he looks at my feet and then into my eyes, I recognize my retreat. I underestimated him. He's much smarter than I am, more cunning, will more easily make money, and will probably be less stressed while doing so. He will not need a corporation to work for. I am impressed, but don't want to admit it. I continue listening to him describing his potential storefront, and the terminology that will follow his name on the door: Christopher Fallswell, Certified Dream Counselor.

My wife's dad, over ninety, frail and sharp, with a daily crossword and walking and phone call routine, finds Chris and me in the foyer. He says, "What type of music is it you play!"

Chris says, "Klezmer music. And mid-period Neil Young and standards. We're open."

The old man takes his hand off Chris's shoulder and says, "Okay," and walks away with the champagne I handed to him to take into the kitchen. Chris and I follow the grandpa at a distance because we both want a drink but also don't want to upset him or speak with him any more than we have to. Chris sees Ann in her eye patch and watches her walk over and grab my arm. He says, "Do you both surf?"

.31% of the population of Connecticut was identified as "American Indian and Alaska Native alone" as of the 2010 Census. A little over ten thousand people. Or is it that a little over ten thousand people self-identified themselves in this way? No matter. I could not find statistics on dream counselors, or even a useful definition of what a "dream counselor" is. If the career is one of Chris's invention, I'm glad.

I took a picture that night in Connecticut of Ann and Chris with their arms around each other, smiling wide. Her patch against his tattoo. It's on my desk now. I'm looking at it. It's evidence of something. Maybe not evidence that can stand against a holstered gun in a grocery store. I don't think that is a relationship that exists in the world: photographs of people > violence. If the link exists and is being won by photographs, the victory is glacial in its reveal and we'll all be shot dead before we can celebrate.

But I don't think that speed proves anything either. Our niece broke up with Chris before moving anywhere with him. She is living at home. Tonight Ann and I will make popcorn and watch cartoons, something bright and moral, the strongest false indicator available that deep down we both know we'll live forever. And if we're lucky later on, Ann will straighten, mute the TV, and we'll listen as the neighbors scream their awful grievances at each other, as our safe chewing slows.

No Door

You leave work five hours late. Your wife knows, you texted her at lunch, you texted her all day, like every day. She says, *I'll be in bed. Try not to wake up J.* You stand in your cubicle and then sit back down because there's nothing else to do.

It's raining. The car is fogged up and you hold your phone to your ear while driving, full volume, because you lost your headphones and want to listen to a podcast about why Trump won't win. It's comforting. But not really. When you park in the driveway you push the car door closed trying to make as imperceptible a sound as possible. The garage is too noisy for this time of night, for Joey, who would wake up and scream if he heard its rumbling. You go in the front. You make your way slowly up the stairs, past the laundry, and past Joey's bedroom. The cat does not meow. You are embarrassed about owning a cat.

You get into bed and your wife whispers, "You lock the door?"

Now, you definitely locked the car, you remember trying the handle after pushing the door closed, but you were so focused on being quiet when coming in, it seems possible, very possible, you did not lock the front door.

You consider a realistic worst case scenario and are immediately troubled that the word you plugged in before "worst case scenario" was "realistic." Because of all the words to place before "worst case scenario," "realistic" is the most terrifying. A less scary/bloody/rape-y/murder-y/cage in the basement-y word would have been "likely." Because at least with "likely" you are remembering all the days when you and your family have slept peacefully and awoken the next morning marred only by your own drool and imaginations, all that daily fading as you and your son stand sleepily near your wife eating her cereal, making faces in the small kitchen. But do past events (non-events) dictate future events (non-events)? You will have that question in your head for less than a day and never arrive at an answer.

A question you are able to answer is whether or not you locked the front door. You could get out of bed now and check, it would be so easy, but you won't. And you could check the camera, FRONT 2, from your phone and see if you stalled at the door as you came in. The system you purchased does not have zoom capabilities from your phone, you'd have to get out of bed and check on the computer for the zoomed information, but, again, you won't do it. And if you were going to get up and check on the computer, scrutinize pixels, you might as well just go downstairs and check the fucking door. But why are you so angry? There's a principle here, somewhere. Why are you angry now and why have you been angry all day, all week? Something has changed, you know it, you feel it, but inside yourself there are only questions.

And it occurs to you as your wife whispers, "Seriously, did you lock the door?" that there is no relation between the safe nights you and your family of three plus the cat have spent here in this house and locking the door. That your safety, your family's safety, is a result of nothing, a result of no door at all. If someone, or some *thing*, wanted to get in the house, get to your family, they would find a way regardless of any door. But you can't say this at 2 a.m. to your wife who is just asking a reasonable question. Especially considering that you forget to do this kind of thing often. So you can't say what you'd like to say, "It doesn't matter," but you want to make your point, want there to be some tangible application of your new belief that locking the door has nothing to do with your family being alive, and so instead you ask, "What kind of question is that?" And you repeat your question, because she says nothing, and you see, of course, she's already asleep.

Tom's Wrong

His primal drunken thought had been: she will not be able to leave me. Tom was prone on the ground blocking the exit path of a vehicle deceitfully similar to his own. This was outside a housewarming party, a second home, Massachusetts by-the-sea. Tom was awoken by a pleading husband whose faded wife was lurking. He eventually allowed himself to be rolled to safety, hands up, as if being unwound from sheets. Big joy for Tom after the unwinding, staring up at the swirling sky. His wife, Julie, could easily have left him there next to the driveway, but did not, calmly emerging from the party and the small crowd watching from the bright porch, finding Tom spread-eagled next to the new mailbox bearing the hosts' hyphenated name. She knelt carefully in her short yellow dress, dropping to one knee, placing her hand on his chest.

Julie drove them to a McDonald's, ordered a plain hamburger for herself and coffee for Tom. She ate the hamburger quickly, taking small bites. She talked to Tom as he tried to sober up, "I was watching you. You had your chin tucked to listen, maintain eye contact, focus. Really trying. I could see the wheels spinning. You were thinking: another party at someone's house. Catered. Tall-backed chairs. Twiggy sticks in vases. I could see you thinking: why?" Tom sometimes loved listening to her talk.

There had been oddness at the dinner party too, starting with the placement of guests at the table. The couples not only had been split, but so had the sexes. Men at one end, women on the other. Tom thought it was the strangest and most exciting seating arrangement imaginable. He lauded it privately watching the group separate. Another man, who couldn't seem to speak without raising his eyebrows and putting a hand to his face said, "Makes judgment plain," nodding at the female half of the room. Tom dashed his praise of the seating chart and shook his head "No" at the man, walking away to hide out in a dim hallway that led to a locked door. Tom downed his drink and tried the handle again. He looked up at an inert red light on a motion detector, wondering what of his movements had been registered.

Julie shone, dressed up slightly more than either of the women flanking her. She was alone in yellow. Tom saw both Julie's seatmates settle into their chairs, watching her conspicuously, until they realized, independently, that she was content to politely ignore them. Julie's focus was elsewhere; her eyes dropped. Tom watched another woman in yellow pass behind Julie, grazing Julie's shoulder with her fingers. Julie was making a concerted effort to demurely neglect this other woman in yellow, wearing *her* dress, her *same* dress.

Tom was unaware of his wife's Naeem Khan purchase, unaware of the dress itself until he saw it in duplicate in front of him. He'd only noticed the color. But here it was younger and sauntering, on a willing, dewy woman that was not his wife. He looked to Julie when he realized this dress was not just similar, but an exact copy. Julie's eyes were closed, her hands somewhere beneath the table. Clenched, he imagined.

Julie's dress double chatted on the periphery with the host-wife, holding a sweating glass of Sauvignon Blanc. The double's boyfriend was running very late. Somehow this information had been completely disseminated throughout the rather hushed party. Tom imagined his wife's double to be speaking faux-humbly about the dress, revealing it was from the designer's ready-to-wear collection, "not runway." Tom had the words, surprising himself with the terminology. So many of the shows were clothes now. Anyone with a TV on the right channels would have the words. Imagined her double possessing descriptors Julie wouldn't have been able to confidently assign: slim racer bodice. It seemed to Tom that the double wanted to be the last to the table, to be given the night's ownership of the dress. On both it was an elegant halter top, sheer glistening and gauze-like to the bust. Yellow. Form fitting, above the knee, but not rigid. The doppelganger was younger, unmarried, and had deftly reapplied her red lipstick in the open more than once, no mirror. Julie was watching her mouth. Everyone was watching her mouth.

At McDonald's Tom was on coffee three, thinking about a celebratory cruise. Nowhere near sober. If he stopped drinking now, he'd only have twelve months to go for a full clean year. That'd be something to celebrate. The view from the back of the ship. The wake spreading, settling. He felt they never did anything together as a couple. Maybe it was that the party had been near the coast. He could imagine a cruise. The startling height of a docked ship charging the whole journey with promise. He was unable to tell Julie how a ship's height was related to mystery, and hope. They'd find another outwardly skeptical couple, huddled at a table near the back for the nightly revue. All reminding one another, often, that they were in the middle of the ocean. Laughing with them, explaining his sobriety as the others ordered more drinks, maybe accepting a clutch of pills from the stranger wife as he led her to the bathroom he'd already visited. "I drink so much more water now," Tom would say.

Tom's Wrong

Julie had her white hamburger wrapper balled up in front of her. She was looking out the window at a baby having a fit in a stroller. The baby's parents were passing a cigarette back and forth and squeezing the baby's feet. It was unclear if any of the cars in the lot belonged to the couple. Out loud, but to no one in particular, Julie said, "Why's that baby here?"

Tom asked, "A year from now, will you take a cruise with me?"

"What?" she asked.

In the car, Julie was shaking her hands out like she'd walked through a summer spider web, bouncing in the passenger seat. It wasn't clear to either of them why Tom was driving. Everything outside was a void until another car would flare up and pass. It was a damp two-lane highway, coastal, mid-summer. Northeastern and lushly rural between towns. Had they been walking it would have seemed entirely blue. A last full blue mistaken for black. That color was lost to them though because they were not, not ever, walkers.

"What is it?" Tom asked.

"I'm just more bothered than I'd like to be that someone else was wearing my dress. I know how silly it is."

"Just stop then," Tom said.

Julie watched the side of Tom's head until he looked at her, and when he turned back to the road, she did not stop staring.

"Enough about the dress. Be done with it," Tom said, lowering his eyes at the road ahead of him.

When they were home, Julie clipped past the babysitter in her heels, their daughter, Rae, clasping and holding on to Julie's leg as she went. Like a slow train picking up mail. Julie's way of not talking to the babysitter had been to say, "Bathroom," in a wobbly, needy voice. A voice unlike any Tom had heard in the car. Tom stood looking at the babysitter on the couch. He was proud of himself for not being attracted to her in that moment. The house had gone quiet. The shower came on, audibly, and Rae's peal of laughter at being allowed to get in. Rae was five.

Lanie, the redheaded babysitter, would have been beautiful if not for her dull, half-lidded eyes. She said it was a chromosomal deficiency. Explained this to clients up front, to waiters, teachers, the dentist, to herself in the mirror. She was open with her diagnosis, because it was truly that noticeable. She looked high, in the immediate and universal sense of the definition.

"Tell the Mrs. I liked her hair tonight," Lanie said.

The babysitter often commented on Julie's hair. She openly lusted after it. She routinely went snooping in the master bedroom's shower looking for the products Julie used and found none. A bar of pale green soap. Stood barefoot in their standup shower and spun, as if a hidden panel's edge would ultimately manifest, the compartment stocked with sumptuous hair supplies. Amber colored gels, golden and backlit. Julie worked in the charitable fund-raising department for a large, but second-tier, mass-market cosmetics and soap products company. The babysitter had told Tom once as he drove her home that she assumed Julie's hair processes and components were secret, that she hid her products and that maybe after a woman was hired into the company, gained enough years, she was given the necessary shampoos, conditioners, leave-in treatments. The babysitter said it was possible she read too exclusively about witches. That her thinking was colored and malformed by secrecy, potion, female control. Tom had not known how to respond and brought up the possibility of opening a distillery, obliquely referencing an impending windfall. Lanie mentioned a potential licensure problem, and Tom pretended to not have heard her.

Early on, Lanie had asked Julie directly what she used in her hair and gotten the truth, though she did not believe it: "Irish Spring. All of us have some awareness of our company's deceit on the shampoo bottle. The 'three ingredient' hand soap. Lies. Veiled by green marketing. I throw away samples and advance promotional items in a dumpster behind the Walgreen's in Maynard. Oh, no. Don't read too deeply, dear."

Lanie blinked slowly.

"Irish Spring," Julie said.

Lanie still casually searched the master bathroom each time she was in the house alone.

Tom and the babysitter could hear singing coming from the shower upstairs. No doors had been closed. The song was being invented on the spot. It was, let's say, called "Tom's Wrong," sung to the tune of "Amazing Grace." Rae knew her dad as Dad, so she sang along without conscious indictment. Julie had a beautiful voice and by reducing "Amazing Grace" down to a two-word lyric, had made the song somehow impossibly stronger.

"You're in trouble," the babysitter said.

Tom tried to guess at how true the babysitter's assessment was. He'd dismissed his wife's reaction about the dress completely after she'd tolerated him passing out drunk in the host's yard at a dinner party. He thought, yes, certainly in trouble.

Tom handed the babysitter forty dollars, and then another twenty. He scanned his living room as if its contents had been somehow adjusted. He couldn't locate what was missing. "I'd appreciate it if what is happening right now stayed—" Tom stopped because the babysitter was nodding her understanding. Tom felt he could trust

Lanie. She was already familiar with the locked guest room containing several hundred of Julie's unworn items. She knew Rae had toilet issues that complicated play dates and naps and basic hygiene. She was familiar with Tom's drinking and non-drinking. Had often babysat Rae while Tom was in the basement "giving time to his own projects." A former roaming Boston Public Schools art therapist for twelve years, recently replaced by a poppy Lesley graduate with a new M.A., Tom could maintain "projects" without much explanation required. But "projects" meant drinking. Lanie had told Tom the house was calmer when he was drunk and Julie was allowed to act unchallenged. Tom hadn't understood he'd ever posed a challenge.

The singing was growing in volume. Rae came out onto the landing, dripping water, her arms raised like a gospel singer, giving a long distance stereo effect to the tune her mother was also keeping time to back in the shower. Her wet hair curling at its ends. Tom imagined Julie had her eyes closed in the shower, trying to project her voice most pointedly, possibly not realizing Rae had left her side.

Tom and the babysitter watched Rae singing, naked and wet, Rae's eyes closed now, maybe remembering her mom's form in the shower. Nakedness was not new to the babysitter. Naked Rae was normal. Had Lanie been alone, she would have found a towel to wrap the girl in. But, with Tom there, she had to stand by for his stunned parenting.

The babysitter closed her eyes and yawned, folding the extra twenty into her bag, next to the bar of soap she'd stolen from the upstairs shower, wrapped in tissue paper.

Rae drifted back towards the shower. The babysitter was old enough to drive but did not. Tom walked up to the master bedroom, following his daughter's wet footprints and said he was taking the babysitter home. He motioned calmly with both hands for them to keep it down, to please stop with the singing. Neither wife nor daughter acknowledged him directly, though their song did trail off. Rae had started to run the bath, sticking a foot into the stream, spraying water and squealing at the freedom she had in the babysitter/parent handoff stage. Julie was leaning against the back glass wall of the standup shower, its door open, lathering her hair with a bar of soap she'd taken from the bathtub. She did not allow her company's products in the house.

The babysitter put on her seatbelt slowly. She patted her bag at her feet. The night was balmy and thick. The trees leaning over the street were swaying heavily. "What's Tom wrong about tonight?" Lanie asked.

"Another woman at the party was wearing Julie's dress." Tom was not far from forgetting what he'd actually done wrong.

"Same yellow dress," she said, "You're wrong how?"

"Julie thought I was watching the other woman," Tom lied, turning to the babysitter and smiling like he thought a dad should in the situation. He especially wanted to seem like a dad, a man changed, to the babysitter. He knew she knew most of the work they'd given her was so he could be drunk in the basement watching the Mets on his computer. And he also sensed she knew that "watching the Mets on his computer" only meant what it sounded like about a quarter of the time.

"Replace what has already happened tonight with something more memorable," she said. "Stub your toe, you break your arm. And you forget the toe."

"I don't think that is how it goes. And, within your analogy, my arm is already broken," Tom said.

The babysitter watched Tom with a sleepy look that made him feel more alone in his problems. Passage of time occurred to him: he could no longer babysit for money, sing naked and wet on landings in front of guests, could no longer effectively imitate his mother in a room, much less a shower. He could no longer do any of these things, although he also never had. And yet, in a year there would be a cruise. Tom imagined ascending the ramp onto the ship at dusk. Magnificently dotted with light. A celebration of the passage of a type of life. Of so much drunk time exchanged for clean, bright, long hours. Earned hours. Tom became aware of the car idling. Lanie did not offer more of her thinking. She appeared to have given her thoughts completely. Tom wasn't ready to drive again. He wasn't sure how he'd gotten them home earlier or why he'd been allowed to drive. His head lolled forward and he jerked upright, repositioning himself in his seat. Tom squinted into the night ahead of him. He felt an important something had not been reached.

"Let me take this," Lanie said, beginning to slide behind the steering wheel. Tom got out of the car and walked around to the passenger seat. They pulled away. Tom held his hands in his lap.

"More memorable. More memorable," he said, in a way that sounded like an attempt to stay awake. Tom was searching for what this could mean, tangibly, as they drove towards the turnpike. Trees, a lack of streetlights and the dark warm night prevented any panorama. The roads leading from their neighborhood, a term unused in this town, were all without sidewalks and were repaired with great tangles of road tar.

The babysitter had her phone out as she drove, texting, picking her head up as they merged towards Boxborough. "You could come with me, where I was going," she said.

Tom declined perfunctorily, and was proud of this response; it felt like a first step, the beginning of his new year. Lanie got out under the hotel portico and went inside to where her sister worked. And in a trance Tom drove home thinking of something like an apology that would be worthy of waking up Julie for.

Tom placed his hands on Julie's shoulders and she took in a breath, waking. She turned her body towards him but did not open her eyes.

"I was thinking we could talk to Lanie about a cruise, watching Rae, coming along and helping. That would work," Tom said, "We'd have time just us."

"Too late," Julie said, her eyes still closed. She turned back to sleep.

And Tom let it go, because he still had a year, and he went downstairs and then downstairs again to begin the project. There were Alaskan cruises. Bahamian cruises. Cruises, he was sure, he'd never even heard of yet.

Wolf Is a River in Germany

Wolf is a river in Germany. On the river's shore in the Black Forest in the German state of Baden-Württemberg is the town of Oberwolfach. The town is nestled in a deep green valley. Its homes and shops are largely indistinguishable from one another: painted white, peaked red shingle roofs. Photographs of Oberwolfach could easily be mistaken for being of a village in the Alleghenies. And in this seemingly familiar town in Germany is the Mathematical Research Institute of Oberwolfach.

The institute looks like a country club compound built by NASA. The way the place was explained, in a conversation I overheard on a nearly empty flight from Omaha to Seattle, was "it's like the Santa Fe Institute, but just math." All I know about the Santa Fe Institute is people like Cormac McCarthy and Sam Shepard take up residence, attend lectures on subjects such as physics inspired approaches to understanding big data, eat lunch with scientists, and retire to their provided work spaces to construct their own fictions.

The Mathematical Research Institute of Oberwolfach explains itself in this way:

In mathematical research, interchange of ideas plays a central role. The high degree of abstraction of mathematics and the compact way it is presented necessitate direct personal communication. Although most new results are nowadays quickly made available to the mathematical community via electronic media, this cannot replace personal contact among scientists.

The MFO (abbreviated from the German: Mathematisches Forschungsinstitut Oberwolfach) does not seem interested in harboring famous writers, any writers. It's possible the MFO could get the German equivalent to Shepard out for a tour, but I have my doubts that such a man even exists, and if he does, I doubt he would be of use to the MFO. The German institute does not appear to value interdisciplinary study in the same way as the American institute. Mathematicians and scientists are welcomed to the MFO, but not musicians, painters. The MFO uses the words "mathematician" and "scientist" interchangeably. This was going to be a story about an American man, not a mathematician, who travels to the MFO, is given a brief residency and—who knows? That might still happen. Though, I see now, all I wanted was

to begin a story with the line "Wolf is a river in Germany."
If anything, it should be the opening line of a song:

Wolf is a river in Germany
And Dodge is the name of a car
Your grandpa, he needed a middle name
Raising his head, that's what he saw
John Dodge Ribery, a name given, yes, but made too
Everything, darling is real: willed or shining through
Everything, darling is real: willed or shining through

"…this cannot replace personal contact among scientists."
Among scientists, he gets it; he's not invited. But if he was.
He arrives in Wayfarers, Wranglers, boots, holding a guitar
case. Poses for a picture in front of the gleaming silver
institute with the Leibniz Fellows, with the Director, and
with Helmut Breithaupt, the caretaker. Helmut has never
been dragged into one of these photos, but the visitor is
insistent. Clearly an ignorant American. Ignorant in all
relevant subjects. His ignorance and nationality are
separate issues. More people on the board than he
would've liked seem to know he initiated contact, via
email: *"What I have to offer the institute is the presentation*
of a concept I use in the process of my songwriting that I think
of as 'decisive unknowing.' The constant inclusion of suppo-
sitions in the writing of narrative pop music. This is more
than lacking a plan and different than choosing arbitrarily
what to write down. I am saying this is consciously not

knowing, and embracing any decision as a viable path. By 'decision' I mean 'sentence' and by 'sentence' I mean 'lyric' and by 'lyric' I mean 'word.' This is a form of decisive abstraction from the narrative already existing in the half-made song, but also an abstraction that forms said narrative. This purposeful unknowing will not be unfamiliar to mathematicians and I will pay my own airfare and will need only lodging. I am asking for a venue to play a free show for your faculty, a meal or two. I will bring postcard-sized handouts with information on how to digitally obtain my latest record 'Labrador Chronicle.' And so if you have a card table for the postcards too. My schedule is open from June to August. Fall is negotiable."

The man's website had been surprisingly coherent, the music American-strange enough, foreign enough, for the board to approve a fifteen-minute time slot on a lark, as long as he was not allowed to give anything resembling a presentation, and understood he was to play three songs and be done. The man would be provided an office with an air mattress for two nights, the dormitory would be full in July, and he would be invited to join the faculty and residents for meals in the cafeteria, free of charge.

I finish an abbreviated set on a small stage in an atrium near the front of the institute. The mathematicians politely clap and some nod encouragingly. There are three men with squarish front teeth laughing, but I choose to believe they are happy. My performance was brief, briefer than promised, because I've been double booked with a presentation by a former VfB Stuttgart Youth Director. He has bushy white eyebrows and blinks hard often. He waits alertly to give his talk in a red and white jumpsuit identical to what the current VfB Stuttgart first team wears in training. When I was singing, he nodded along to my music without expression. I take this as a compliment. His talk is not translated from the German, but his passion is evident. I imagine he is explaining how identifying athletic talent in young men is instructive in other identification quandaries in life. He might believe speed can't be taught, though I am not certain how this would translate outside of sport. I'm guessing he said "sport" and not "sports." After the former youth director's talk he gives me a thumbs up, I'm assuming for the music, which he didn't have to do. I return his gesture. There is a hurrah from the mathematicians for our moment of mutual admiration.

I'd asked for a card table for my postcards, but apparently "card table" doesn't translate. I lay out my postcards on the edge of the stage after the soccer talk is finished. But, the mathematicians do not linger in the atrium, and most everyone starts filing outside into the summer day, onto the grassy expanse in front of the institute that provides a view down into the valley. One would have to shield his eyes and search to pick up the movement of a car in the town below. Inside with me, a longhaired male faculty member, wearing a thick leather bracelet on each wrist, approaches the stage and picks up a postcard. He looks at the cover art for *Labrador Chronicle* depicted on the postcard, and asks, "Labrador, as in dog?" I'm guessing he has to ask because there is no dog on the album's cover. Instead, there is a photograph of a child dressed as a cowboy slumped in a car seat.

I say, "No, Labrador, as in wolf," trying to formulate a joke.

And he frowns, "Wolf means wolf in Germany. Labrador is dog. The office we provided for you is next to my own office. Please do not consider playing your guitar."

I maintain eye contact with the longhaired, leather cuffed man, wanting him to know our talk, the one we are having, is among scientists, and I would not break that bond. I push a postcard into his chest and tell him, "I know that's not what you really wanted to say."

For Carl

If you are familiar with what a buffalo looks like in profile, then I can describe what it was to see Carl stepping out of his pearl blue Dodge Shadow as the snow began to fall. Namely, a buffalo seen at some distance, apart from the herd, dropping and raising its head. The snow was wind-whipped and nothing was sticking yet, so the empty high school parking lot just looked slicked by rain. It was our old school; we'd graduated nine years earlier. The snow stung my face as I watched Carl tug at his clothes and relocate me in his field of vision. He opened his mouth, tongue out for a snowflake. I turned to shield myself from the cold gusting, winced. I felt stupid for not insisting on another meeting place. Somewhere indoors.

This is not going to be about Carl's weight gain over the period of time in which I didn't see him, and it is not going to be about why we were not in contact. It's not going to be about Carl's contraction of Cushing's syndrome as a result of taking glucocorticoid steroids while recovering from a pancreas transplant. Not going to be about why I was home in Colorado or why I would soon be leaving. Well, about that, I'll just say quickly that my mom's ancient corgi, Jackie Coogan, had died and she was struggling. But, no, actually, none of that is going to enter greatly; instead, this is going to be a story of the favor that Carl needed from me. The favor he needed in the winter of 2013, after not seeing me in close to ten years and while in the interim contracting a rarish condition, from steroids, that caused him to look like a buffalo. With a hump and a heavily jowled face and a belly hanging. And here he was, lumbering from his car, bracing as the wind hit him too, to give me what I recognized late to be a hug.

We'd known each other in high school because Carl and I were on the wrestling team together, in a sense. For reasons purportedly medical, Carl's parents had not allowed him to wrestle. But even then, we all knew diabetes was not cause enough to be forbidden from high school athletics. With uncharacteristic solemnity the whole wrestling team respected Carl's decision to penitentially serve as team assistant. He helped us wipe down the mats to prevent the spread of ringworm. He tried to run laps with us, barking encouragement from yards behind when he slowed to a walk. He traveled with us to meets, dressed in our team windsuit, and cheered like a man possessed. And I want to be clear: that was Carl consistently. Not just at his best, or from the top of my memory.

For Carl

He was doggedly who he was. And we looked to him despite not knowing we were doing so.

I came out of Carl's grip and again took in the Dodge. It was very well kept for being such a forgotten and undesirable model. This was not a car he'd had in high school. There had been no car in high school. Carl was smiling at me from close range.

Like his car, Carl was in blue, and very intentionally, a Buffalo Bills jacket with the old red standing buffalo logo over his heart. He'd always forefronted that which could be turned against him. If he looked like a buffalo, by God, he'd wear it on his chest. Once, after a meet, all of us at some laxly parented house, I'd seen him ease into a sexual relationship with a mostly silent girl by simply announcing his shortcomings as an introduction, "You think you aren't interested in the fat kid, pug nose, and let's say it, maybe you're not—" Carl turned and looked at his car with me.

He said, "Let me guess what you're thinking here: Now, Dodge Shadows were taken out of production in 1994, but it seems beyond Carl's luck to have the latest possible, so it is my guess that this car is probably close to a 1989. At the latest. But all those Shadows were pretty similar, so, I could have that wrong. Well. You're almost right. It's a 1991."

I checked my pockets for my keys and phone, as if missing either would somehow mean I'd be long stranded. "Where do you want to do this?" I asked.

"I'd like to get food," he said.

I made turns behind Carl that had at one time been held in my muscle memory. A left out of the high school onto Arapahoe. Arapahoe to Parker Road and Parker Road until we were traveling through the in-between place before the town of Parker actually began. On the brown hills to our left were old spread-out housing developments whose residents would have shuddered at being said to live in a neighborhood, homes purchased in the seventies by people with ragged horses and dreams of ranches, dreams now dashed by living in sight of a Costco, a toll-driven highway, two hospitals and plenty of efficiently healthless dining options. Thick carpets and Labradors and old Cherokees and Broncos and Silverados, hateful football and tourism opinions, mostly non-natives who would dread their actual birthplaces being widely known. Small liberal art school graduates who aligned themselves with a Big 8 member, then begrudgingly ended up watching Pac-12 ball. And with increasing conference pollution, their weekends became aimless, lost ritual. These angry residents were for the most part gone. I was projecting the families I was familiar with on these hills, these houses. But they had been there. And now there were Californians who believed the current state of the neighborhood to be well within their rural ambitions. Their houses faced west, as my childhood home did, and they did have a view. No doubt. Mountains and the nightly leak of headlights through the crack in the range that was I-70 eastbound. Growing up with a view ruined me for many other places with lesser vistas. Places like Fort Worth and the ninth floor of Radio Shack corporate headquarters.

Carl chose Waffle House. We were greeted by the shout of the waitresses' breakfast code as we entered, "Pull one bacon, half sausage, drop two hash brown, one in a ring. Mark order scrambled plate." We took a booth and were accosted by the waitress, who before anything else wanted to know if we would need any "other additional hot sauces," to which Carl said, "Please, yes."

I regret the way I started. It's true, Carl looked like a buffalo, maybe still does, that wasn't a misrepresentation. But, I also could have opened by mentioning *I* initiated contact with Carl. My first day home had been spent drinking tea and playing cribbage with my mom and walking a mall while attempting to shield her from the sight of all dog media. I'd tried to think of who might still be in town. The internet offered up whole networks of people I didn't want to see. So I'd called and told Carl I was home for a few days. He sounded pleased, but unsurprised. He asked about Texas, if I still followed wrestling on any level, I didn't, if I was still a Broncos fan, I was, asked about a wife or girlfriend, none. He told me about the pancreas transplant. How it might, in part, cure him of his diabetes. Heard about his Cushing's and how the doctors weren't willing to begin radiation and chemo to get rid of it this soon after his surgery. He was only a month and a half out. He'd have to live with it for a while. And maybe because I couldn't come up with anything to say, Carl offered, "There's something you can do for me."

I nodded. From the Waffle House booth, I could see a construction rental outfit, a greenhouse, and a strip with an Old West facade that held a tattoo parlor, gun shop and a Catholic store. The snow had stopped and the day was beginning to blue. There was a dark, purplish suggestion of mountains on the horizon.

Carl said, "I received a present from a woman, a woman I work with, teach with, one of the other seventh grade science teachers and it's unclear to me if it is a crucible—"

"Say 'test,'" I told him.

"It is unclear to me if the present is a crucible or merely the opening of a relationship," Carl said. From his Bills jacket Carl produced an envelope. Inside was a gift certificate for something called Spacetime Flotation.

"Sensory deprivation tanks. Pitch dark, soundless tank. You float in skin temperature saltwater. People use it to quell insomnia, stress, et cetera," Carl said.

I couldn't believe he said "quell." I asked, "Why is this just not a gift?"

"Because she knows I am afraid of the dark," Carl said, and before I could ask, he said, "I told her I was afraid of the dark."

I agreed to go float for Carl. I was surprised I had an opportunity to be of some use in his life. I mean, Jesus, it was all mounting up on him. Diabetes, pancreas transplant, Cushing's; it all seemed the prelude to a phone call bringing news of his death. A hypothetical phone call I would receive from my mom. That being said, I'm not positive that news of Carl's death would actually reach her. Even if she were told of his passing, Carl's name would not be one she'd ever known.

The next morning I called Spacetime Floatation.

"Your first time with us? A few things then. We recommend no caffeine in the three hours leading up to your visit, helps with focus. We recommend not shaving just before your visit. The saltwater can burn a little. And, eat. A float is not ideal if you are hungry. Lastly, I'm going to need a credit card, because we do charge a $50 cancellation fee if the cancellation occurs less than 24 hours before your scheduled visit."

"I'm making an appointment for this afternoon. In a few hours."

"Exactly. Exactly. So, I'll take your credit card number when you are ready."

Spacetime Floatation was a business run out of an industrial park. Like youth gymnastics or small time manufacturing or batting cages. There was a roll up garage door open, and inside the empty concrete floored space was an office door, with "S.F.F." stenciled on the glass, that led to a low-lit lobby and tall counter, all reminiscent of a dermatologist's office. On the coffee table next to a stack of homeopathic remedy magazines was a Himalayan salt lamp, glowing pink. A four-foot wide aquarium with brightly colored fish was set in the wall. Some of the volumes on the bookshelf: *Endurance: Shackleton's Incredible Voyage*, *The Sufi Path of Love: The Spiritual Teachings of Rumi*, *Mega Brain*, *Athletic Massage*. The smell in the lobby was Nag Champa, and was powerful enough to divorce my thoughts from the industrial park, Carl, buffalos, the dog Jackie Coogan and all the rest that had led up to me entering the lobby.

A woman stood from behind the counter and said my name. She had her thick blonde hair pulled back in a ponytail and was wearing a plain blue T-shirt and khaki shorts. I had a flash that she had at one time been in a cult, walking between dusty cabins in a cotton dress with a doily collar, that she had followed a lanky, charismatic leader.

That she'd been fooled. I had the feeling she was from Texas.

"Is there someone floating back there right now?" I asked.

"Yes, but you don't have to see him if you don't want to."

I wasn't worried about that, but I said, "If that's ok, I'd prefer not to."

The woman said her name was Skylar and handed me a clipboard with a form to complete. The purpose of your visit: –Physical Therapy –Meditation –Stress Relief –Insomnia –Focus/Creativity –Relaxation –Other. I tried to think what would be the most honest response for Carl. Maybe the woman who bought him the gift certificate wanted him to relax in light of his medical problems, or sleep better, or, really any of the options seemed appropriate. They all struck me as related. I put an X next to "Meditation," because I felt it had the lowest probability of generating follow up questions.

Skylar told me she'd be a few minutes longer in preparing my room and the tank. I looked around the lobby trying to hold on to details to repeat for Carl, even began enumerating how many yellow fish, how many electric blue, but stopped myself, realizing I'd have enough for him to appear convincing.

Skylar led me to the room with the float tank. The room was just as low-lit as the lobby. The tank was against the far wall, and at the near end of the tank was a shower basin and ceiling mounted showerhead. The tank was the shape of a broad and tall coffin with one end forming a slope where the door was. On the tank was a small wooden platform with a clean towel, a package of earplugs, and cotton swabs.

Skylar watched me take in the room. She stood in the shower basin in her shoes and gave me the following spiel in the style of a veteran flight attendant, "This is a Samadhi Float Tank. The door, you can see here, is very light. Five pounds. Since this is your first time I recommend you put your head at the far end of the tank, nearest the air filtration system, and have your feet at the door. To get out, at any time during your float simply push against the door. The water in the tank is 94.6 degrees Fahrenheit, average skin temperature, and in the water is 800 pounds of dissolved Epsom salt. You are used to gravity pressing down on you all day, every day, and sometimes first time floaters after reclining will attempt to hold their heads up, thus putting unneeded stress on their necks. Place your hands behind your head if need be. Relax into the water, it will rise to just above your ears, hence the earplugs, though saltwater is harmless if it does enter your ear canal, but know, the saltwater *will* buoy you. Before you get in the tank, rinse off, and make sure to dry your face thoroughly. If your face is wet, droplets will form while you are in the tank and you will want to brush them off. Problem is, your hands will be covered in saltwater, salt could potentially get in your eyes, your mouth, et cetera. These are distractions we don't want. When your time is up I will come and knock on the door to the room twice, if I don't hear a response, I will flip this light," Skylar flipped a switch by the door and the room became completely red, "That way if you think you heard a knock at any time during your float and open the door to the tank and find the room is *not* red, you will know that you imagined the knock. If you open the door and find the room red, please get out of the tank and take your shower. If I knock on the door, flip the light, and do not hear the shower come on after several minutes, I will again knock on the door to the room and then enter if I hear no response and knock on the tank itself. At that point, should we reach it, knock on the sidewall from within the tank so I know you have heard me. Any questions?"

"Naked, right?"

"Yes, naked."

"No questions, Skylar."

In the tank I reclined into the blackness. I spent the hour extending my arms to my side and pushing gently off the inner wall with my pinky, drifting to the other side of the tank at what felt like quarter speed. I thought of a professor I'd had in college, an accounting professor, blonde and shiny, who enthusiastically told me about how waking up daily to read the paper had changed her life.

Routine, she said. Routine from the start of each day. She read one article from every section. That was her secret: not mastery, but building a broad knowledge base. I remember her setting her shoulders back as she said this, maybe noticing me noticing her pink sweater with faux pearl buttons down the front. Shoulders back, "broad knowledge base." I thought about my breathing. Wondered why Skylar had not quite prepared me for how muggy the tank would be. And I had to open the door once during my float because I spun out thinking I was not able to take in a full breath. When I sat up in the tank to open the door, saltwater from my hair trickled down into my left eye, and when I lay back down into the surrounding dark of the tank I squinted my left eye shut and waited for the burn to subside. Which it did. But beyond skipping through thoughts of various women who'd served in authority roles in my life, and attempting to gauge the passage of time, mostly what was occupying my attention was waiting for Skylar's knock. And when it came, I emerged into a red room and took my shower. If anything, all the tank time had made the shower a euphoric, restorative godsend.

I walked out to my car with wet hair and Carl was waiting, standing in front of his Shadow.

"What have you got for me?" he said.

I told him about the lobby, the fish, Skylar, and my impression of her, told him about what books were on the shelf. I mentioned all the procedural elements of entering the float room, the tank and its shape, the close air, how I had to open the door halfway through. How it was difficult to tell how much time had passed, how incredible the shower had felt upon getting out, and Carl stopped me.

"So it's about the shower?"

I felt like since I'd been sent out to gather information, to arrive at "the shower afterwards felt great" was close to failure. Or, failure.

"I don't know if 'it's about the shower,' but—"

"No, no. That's what I'll tell her. 'It's about the shower.' Showers are usually taken in full light, so that's great for me. And easier to replicate, cheaper too, than this sensory deprivation business."

"You feel you have enough to convince her?" I asked.

"If she asks questions I don't have answers for, at that point, should we reach it, I can always get in touch."

I was thrown by Carl's phrasing. It was as if he'd heard Skylar's tank introduction before. And I was a little lost on where Carl was taking the information I'd given him, but it seemed that he'd already incorporated it into his plans. He told me I didn't have to understand, and I believe something close to that. I hope his health improves. And I made sure to say Carl's name several times to my mom before leaving town, so if she hears anything, she can let me know.

Warning

My brother arrives from Chicago with a mustache and a toothache. From a reclined position on our living room couch he enumerates the benefits of being able to walk to the grocery store, the bar, library, to the doctor, the train—

"I lived in Rogers Park for ten years," I tell him. "Please, keep your socks on."

"And now you live in Albuquerque, so I'm reminding you," he says.

"Remind me, why are you here?"

Socks off, my brother throws them, balled, at my head. The ball flies past my ear, lands softly on our wood floor and slides into the kitchen like a low-hovering ghost.

My wife walks into the living room with a look on her face that I take to mean *so this is what your house was like.* She is wearing face paint, two blue lines down each cheek and a series of yellow lightning bolts across her forehead. Her chin appears to have been dipped in a bowl of red. My daughter walks into the room smiling wildly, looking up at her mother as she turns the corner from the kitchen, and her face as she runs between me and my brother I take to mean *Mom looks fucking crazy!*

My wife standing in her paint listens to my brother talk about his toothache. He looks at the ceiling as he talks to us, his arms in the air. I want to tell him the movies he's been watching have been lying to him—but it's unrelated.

"Why did you let him grind it down without taking an X-ray?" she asks.

"When you go to the doctor and he says he wants to give you a shot, do you ask for more proof?" he asks my wife.

"She does," I say. And this is true, she does. I've never seen her accept any suggestion/idea/plan from a stranger without a series of questions, without returning the whole undertaking, whatever it may be, to first principles. My brother has never been with a woman like my wife. Sexually or otherwise. She'd make him sob realizing all he's been missing—that is, if my brother was the type of man who realized things.

"You may just have been stressed and chewing harder than usual. Are you one side dominant when you chew your food?" she asks him. My daughter stands miming the act of shoveling food in her mouth and chewing. She bares her teeth like a dramatic friendly dog.

Warning

I cut in. "Everyone is one side dominant when chewing their food, unless you are a person who readily uses the term 'one side dominant' in regards to chewing food. And even those people—(my wife starts sighing and letting her eyes go cross-eyed)—and even those people familiar with one side chewing problems, I would guess, are by far, *by far*, chewing on one side of their mouths."

My wife mouths the word "fucking" followed by actually saying "Alright!"

My daughter is looking back and forth between her mom and me. My brother is making the same face as my daughter. A face in retreat. My daughter burps, and then burps again, looking dazed. She is wide-eyed; her body is betraying her.

My brother says, "Right side chewer."

My wife is angrier than I understood ten seconds ago. Something about me shouting her down, on this topic, is getting to her. She shouts me down too, often. Sometimes I start days by saying, "Let's have a good day today," like someone in a TV movie, the kind that doesn't get made anymore. Like a stepdad in an old TV movie. But I'm not trying to be funny. I really want to put it out there from the start that no matter what happens, I promise you, I'm trying and know the day before got a little fucked.

She turns to my brother. "So you're stressed. You're champing hard. You're growing a mustache. Out with it. What happened?"

My daughter jumps in front of her uncle and I notice her hands are both completely blue. She puts up her blue hands, "He doesn't have to tell you! You don't have to tell them! They'll remember whatever you say for as long as you live!"

Banking

My wife tells me she's been thinking of a man she used to know. She actually uses the word "boy," but I react at first as if she's said "man." We are eating lunch outside at a fast-casual Mexican restaurant in Phoenix, where we live. It's a newer part of town. This restaurant is not yet a true chain, there are only three in metro Phoenix, but everything about the place is pared, repeatable, set for a buyout. When the obvious comparisons arise, it seems the restaurant's defense is that they do only tacos—regionally authentic constructions, make and bottle their own hot sauce, and sell no soda. One of the three shirt designs for sale at this location reads: "Water and beer. Coffee's next door." I like the shirt, maybe because it confuses me, but would never buy it. In the parking lot near where we're eating are pairs and clusters of business people and radiant young mothers and loud teenagers with unbelievable vehicles.

Cardinal

I've been with my wife since we were in college and heard all her stories, but because she's said "boy" and didn't give a name, I'm thinking this is a person from her distant past. From a time that predates most of the stories she tells. She says, yes, "distant, or, just from when I was a kid," and because we are both only thirty-one years old, I see her point. My wife repeats the word "distant" and squints at me, her face is in the sun and she has pushed the scraps of her taco lunch away from her. She's freckled enough so you'd notice and is wearing denim overalls with a confidence that would make you think she's a painter. That this is down time for her and she'll be returning within the hour to her canvas, a large work in progress. But, she's not a painter. I have the day off from work and my wife makes her own hours. She owns and operates a photo portrait studio with her sister. It's why we moved here. This is my wife's second career, her first being social work when we lived in Chicago, doing cognitive testing on the children who were in the agency's homeless to housing transition program. We moved to Phoenix four months ago and are still catching on. Sunsets, driving, rock lawns, meals outside in February.

My wife says this boy she's been thinking of is a part of her online banking login. I try not to react, but I can see in my wife's face that I have already given myself away. I glance towards the parking lot and watch a woman in a sports bra slam her car door completely without affect. I'd

58

bet the sports bra woman's kitchen is immaculate. I think about the blue cold surfaces she might maintain because I'm not sure how I'd like to continue in the conversation I'm presently in. I'm capable of being simpleminded enough when it comes to my wife that this kind of talk can bother me. Talk of others.

I pull what remains of my wife's lunch to my side of the table and when she doesn't stop me, I eat. The basket's aroma has flattened, but is still wonderfully of lime and roast chicken. Before, in similar situations, concerns over portion control have been voiced and I've been cautioned. Today, I'm allowed to keep eating without comment. She does not appear to take any notice as I finish her meal, though I am certain this is not the case. As if the concept would be foreign, she says, "To get into the account there's two security questions. When I set it up I gave answers for ten or so basic questions, and the two questions I'm asked during each login come from this group, randomly. It's possible I answered only four setup questions initially, or three, and, if that's the case, the fact that I'm always asked, 'What was the name of your childhood best friend? (If your answer is a date, use form mmddyy),' would make a lot more sense. Trevor was his name. Still is, presumably."

"On the joint account the answer to that question is 'Marcy,'" I say.

"There's more than one right answer," she says, and I can't argue with that. My wife tells me a little about

Trevor. She brings the backs of her hands down her cheeks, gesturing, and says, "skinny Slavic face." Her gesture and the word "Slavic" make me think of a long-bearded old man, but I do not repeat "Slavic" back to her questioningly. I listen and try to picture a lanky kid, tough, with an accent, new to the desert like me. She says that Trevor's parents were first generation immigrants from the Czech Republic and moved to Mesa, where my wife is from, in the eighties in order for Trevor, their first child, to be born in the United States. I tell her it's strange to think of her as a girl not knowing the concept of "first generation immigrants," then later learning and applying the term. My wife does not think this is strange at all and continues. Now that I know Trevor was born and raised in Arizona I try and erase an Eastern European accent from my understanding of him, but can't. Trevor, she says, played "travel baseball" as a boy, but got a girl pregnant towards the end of high school and ended up moving to where her family was from in Nevada. I don't see any relationship between "travel baseball" and an unplanned pregnancy. It seems my wife believes Trevor's promising athletic future was negated. It also seems to me that she's shown her hand. She's considered alternate lives for Trevor. Maybe, still does. I watch my wife adjust an overall strap and she says, "Boulder City, Nevada, specifically."

As best I can see it, the outside understanding of why we moved to Arizona was so my wife could switch careers, so we could save money, and so we could, possibly, start to think about having a baby. I don't want a baby. My wife knows it and has always known it, and has maintained that she is content with me solely being "open to the possibility that I could change my mind," which I am. My job allowed for a lateral transfer at the same salary without much difficulty. I'm a middle manager at an art supply store chain. I'll work there until I don't want to anymore, and then I'll do something else. The career switch for my wife, that was a real reason to move, saving money too. Both those understandings from the remaining parents and friends and now ex-coworkers are valid. Her sister is nearby, her mother too. About kids, the decision will, I believe, be taken away from me at some point and there will be a child. That is not imminent though. What is imminent is that my wife is thinking of a man she used to know and I am bothered. I believe this is a good sign.

Cardinal

I am returning four rented tuxedos in San Diego the day after my older brother's wedding. It's late morning, Sunday, bright and green October. I take the 163 out of the city and down, dense with traffic, between verdant tree-topped hills to the broader and browner 8. I get off the highway at the Mission Valley mall with its mass of strip shopping centers, one of which holds the Men's Wearhouse where I am returning the tuxes. In the strip's parking lot a young security guard on a Segway is patrolling. He seems focused on the lot, the parked cars themselves, though I am not sure why.

I am met nearly at the door of the Men's Wearhouse by a round woman in a blazer, who quickly hangs the tuxes on a metal rack for inspection. She takes brisk inventory and says since everything's in the bags, and "No? Don't need a receipt?," that I'm all set. I ask her what the security guard is doing, so fixated on the cars. She tells me his job when the Chargers are at home is to make sure people don't park in the mall lot and then take the trolley out to see the game, avoiding paying for parking at the stadium. She says the stadium, which she calls only "Qualcomm," is a ten-minute trolley ride away. "Do you know him?" I ask, meaning the security guard.

"Luis? Sure. He comes in and drinks the coffee we set out for customers. Friendly guy." The coffee spread is impressive. A stainless steel dual thermal setup. Regular and decaf. Half and half, soy creamer, raw sugar, stevia extract, a few pink Sweet'n Lows, thin red plastic stirrers. And, strangely, Anthora paper cups, the familiar New York Greek diner blue and white. I ask the woman which of the employees is from New York, trying to understand the presence of the cups and she misunderstands me, says, "No, I'm from here."

On the curb, I put my hand over my eyes and watch Luis going through the rows, leaning his Segway in various directions. His job seems difficult to me. Not everyone who is wearing a jersey is going to the game, and not everyone who walks away from the stores is either. Luis appears to be in his early twenties, Latino, over six feet tall and soft looking.

When I approach Luis I ask how he determines when someone is headed to Qualcomm. He points towards the highway, "On the other side of that Best Buy? The one that's blocking our view of the 8 there? That's a Green Line trolley stop. That's south. If I see an individual park in our lot here, and head due south, they are getting towed. It's that simple."

"You're not looking for a jersey or a cap or anything like that?"

"Not concerned with caps or jerseys, no, not even concerned if they are going to the game. Because I've been duped on that front. I started with that approach being a key component as to whether or not I actually made the call for the tow. And I missed a lot of people that way. By being too selective. Now I go by the letter of our posted sign. That this parking lot is for patrons of the stores in this section of the mall, period. If you are headed south out of this parking lot on foot, away from these stores, you are not a patron of these stores—for my purposes. And you get towed. I deal solely in cardinal directions. North, east, west, ok. And another look to see if the person or persons actually enters a store. You were west, with tuxes."

"Right," I say.

"Who got married?" Luis asks.

"My brother."

"You were best man," Luis says. His eyes follow the path of a short bald man departing from his car. Luis drifts on the Segway angling for a better view.

"Not the best man. But, in the wedding," I say to him.

Luis nods, "One of those kind of deals."

I ask if he would want to eat, say that I don't have anyone to eat lunch with. Luis says he could always eat, and that his workday is over in a half hour once the game starts. I walk back inside the Men's Wearhouse, nod at the woman who again meets me at the door, and quietly help myself to the coffee. Another employee in a bowtie is earnestly vacuuming in a corner, holding the looped power cord like a lariat. I sit near the changing rooms watching young men being helped into jackets, and when I am asked, say only that I'm already being helped.

After fifteen minutes or so I walk back outside. Luis is standing next to a late model, white, single-cab Toyota Tacoma. The truck is very clean. The driver side door is open and Luis is changing out of his boots into a pair of sneakers. He pulls on fresh white socks and then tugs the shoes on without undoing the laces. He is taller than the truck. I ask where the Segway went, and he jerks his thumb over his shoulder, meaning back behind the strip, "We have a shed behind a barbwire fence near the generators."

Luis says he'd like to go somewhere he's never been before, and says he'd prefer going somewhere we'd "really have to drive to." He says he wants a hamburger, but wants to pay at least ten dollars. "I need it to be thick enough where they ask how I want it cooked." He begins unbuttoning his white short sleeve shirt, replete with patches and generic groupings of badging, epaulettes. The company he works for is named Cali-Secure. Where it should say "Luis" on his nametag, it says "Cali-Secure." Once he's down to his undershirt and has it untucked he says that we also have the option to just go back to his apartment, and his mom will cook.

"Are you in a rush?" Luis asks. Out of his uniform he seems to have new interest in the day.

"Not at all, not until tomorrow," I say, "I have a dinner later and a plane tomorrow." The parking lot seems to have grown suddenly packed, people darting from their vehicles, but off the clock, Luis seems not to notice.

"Where's your date from the wedding?" Luis asks.

"I didn't get a plus-one. It's a little complicated."

Luis reaches out and lazily knocks on the roof of his truck as he speaks, "You weren't supposed to come. Or they didn't know if it would be appropriate for you to come, or if you would come."

"Yeah. I guess it's not that complicated," I say.

"Sure it is. Just also common. Complicated and common are not mutually exclusive."

Luis's mom is not Latino, but a short black woman with hair that reminds me of Allen Iverson. She is wearing a white collared shirt with the sleeves rolled up, jeans and rainbow colored striped socks. Based on the way she is dressed, it is very difficult for me to know anything about her. I don't say this, but, my understanding of her would be altered greatly if I knew whether or not Luis is adopted.

She is making us gin martinis in the kitchen, out of sight. The martinis, she says, are all the cooking she'll be doing today. "You boys can walk to McDonald's and get a sack of hamburgers for all of us after this first drink, if you're still hungry." She pronounces McDonald's "Mac-Don-ald's," which endears me to her immediately. Also, her belief that we might cease to be hungry is charming somehow.

The apartment is ideal and fairly representative of the older construction in the Bankers Hill neighborhood, north of downtown San Diego. There is a small ruddy courtyard behind a red wrought iron fence. The apartment sits on top of a garage belonging to the owner of the unit, and to reach the front door you must first climb ornate Spanish tiled stairs. The front door faces south and the afternoon light is intense through the broad front window. The ceiling is vaulted and high. In the four upper corners of the bright living room, Oaxacan masks are perched. Other Oaxacan animal carvings: a wide-eyed jaguar and a crow adorn the top of a squat black bookcase full of unfamiliar novels, painting monographs, and biographies of relatively obscure successes. The one that catches my eye is of György Ligeti, the composer. *György Ligeti: Of Foreign Lands and Strange Sounds*. I ask, "Whose apartment is this?" then quickly correct myself when Luis looks at me skeptically, and I ask the question I really want answered, "Whose books are these?"

Luis's mom comes in with the drinks and says, "Our apartment. Our books. You have to be more specific with your questions." I ask about the Ligeti and both say they'd read it. The unified areas of interest between Luis and his mother surprise me. I think of my own mother. Our reading habits are not related. But, I remember her taking me to all the movies I couldn't get into without an adult when I was younger, and a strong emotional reaction from her in the theater always increased my own feelings for the movie. *Adaptation* being the example I can think of most readily. We wept.

"Did you wear that shirt to match your son's uniform?" I ask Luis's mother.

She smiles with her whole face and says, "No, but I like that. Now I might." Her particular flourish with the martinis, she tells me, is a dab of Worcestershire sauce at the bottom of the chilled glass. She says the recipe comes from a New York pilot. She asks what I think of Luis's job. I tell her I like seeing someone who takes his job seriously, and that was what made me interested in Luis at all. His full attention to his job made me want to talk to him.

"Because it was a job that you wouldn't expect the person to be giving his full attention to?" she says.

I start to qualify my original answer and then stop, "Yes," I say, "That must be part of it. And because it seemed difficult."

Both Luis and his mom laugh. Luis says, "Not even— 1:30 in the afternoon? And we're drinking? Not hard."

"But it's Sunday," I say, though this goes unnoticed. A cloud gets in front of the sun and I think of the plane I will take the next day back to the part of the country with weather and my own rote way of paying rent. I drink deeply, but only to catch up. I feel embarrassed for having spoken so freely about Luis's job. Especially since he had the unique decency to welcome me into his home without asking anything of my own work.

Luis's mom is on her feet again, putting on music. There are speakers on either side of the room, but I don't know what the delivery system for the music is. She puts on what I recognize to be *Solo Monk* and this seems to signal that Luis *is* adopted. Seems to signal a certain openness and largeness of heart in this woman.

I try to clarify what I was saying earlier after the music becomes a part of the room, "The other thing was that he had a plan. A whole way of thinking surrounding his job. It seemed so disciplined and logical for what essentially was determining to tow or not tow cars—"

Luis interrupts, "That's for a game day. Or a concert, same thing. Otherwise I am mall security, as you know it—"

His mother interrupts, "Stop. The towing logic *is* his own. He's undermining his invention. He's undermining his own clarity of approach. We found this phrase, 'To orient oneself, it is enough to find a single cardinal direction,' and went from there. Right?"

Luis stands and gives the facial equivalent of a shrug. He calls out from the kitchen, asks if I want another drink. I tell him I can't, that I need my wits about me for tonight. His mother asks when I am expected for dinner. And I tell her that I did everyone a favor this morning by returning the tuxes in hopes that I would be able to arrive late, unquestioned, or not show up at all.

"So, the favor becomes what? Not an alibi. And not an excuse, and it doesn't exactly buy you time in any real way does it? The favor becomes what?"

"Confusing," I tell her, "It becomes confusing."

"It becomes a gesture," she says. "You are gesturing towards caring about these people, about wanting to do right by them, but maybe you aren't actually doing the work of caring about them or doing right by them. You love them, I'm guessing, and do enough to artificially remind them this is the case, and because you let them know this in a small way, deep down you feel they know your love for them in a more permanent way, and this gives you permission to do what you would actually like to do, which is, not keep plans, and drink with strangers and walk around surprised."

Some of what she says is right. I am surprised, flaky. I want to ask her, "What do you do?" but am afraid to, and sense I will, hear of readings, chakras, essences, and end

71

up having her profession inflicted on me even more than it already has been. Instead I ask her about Monk. About other albums of his she admires. But she gives me a blank look.

"This is Luis's music. I just put something on."

Luis comes back into the room holding a new drink. It looks like he's put water in his hair and combed it. I'm thinking of what type of the common California witches Luis's mom might be, a psychic, a healer, and realize I haven't been hungry since being in the apartment. I put a hand on my stomach, and maybe Luis takes this as a sign, because he asks if I would like to go get the hamburgers we'd talked about. I decline and say I should probably be leaving. I thank Luis's mom, who looks annoyed and walks into the other room. Luis walks with me to my car parked on the street.

I want to tell him that moving out might be good for him, but I don't really know if that's true. I don't know what kind of debt he's in, or not, don't know about his health, his strength, anything. We shake hands and laugh, and it's a little awkward, because clearly there is an unreasonable amount of affection between us for how little we know each other. Maybe it is mostly on my end. I get in the car and Luis knocks on the passenger window, which I put down so he can speak to me. "Take me with you," he says, laughing. I laugh too and wave goodbye. I want him to know that he wouldn't have said that had he known the quiet I was headed for, the avoidance and low light and fork scraping. I wish he had said, "Let's leave together."

Before the Reception

The rain was not a surprise. The bride, Jemma Rygaard, had been earnestly attempting to check forecasts for August 15 since the night of her engagement roughly thirteen months previous. Initially, she had to employ general information about seasonal weather in Flagstaff, i.e. average monthly temperature data, as her source, but after more searching she found a website willing to predict weather ninety days into the future. The *90-Day Weather Center* homepage maintained up to the minute accuracy percentage tallies for each of their United States regions of forecasting. Southwestern accuracy had been consistently in the upper 80th percentile since Jemma began paying attention in February. It wasn't clear to her what the specific criteria for determining a prediction's accuracy was, though. The margin of error allowed within an "accurate" prediction was unclear. But, rain *had* been the call from ninety days out, and, yes, she thought and then voiced as she looked out the suite's window at the puddles spreading and linking in the parking lot, "Home run, guys."

It occurred to Jemma she was referring to a website as "guys," and was speaking to these guys; she began laughing, still wearing her wedding dress, as her mother Poll Rygaard poked her head into the room, the door was unlatched, and witnessed her daughter, the bride, laughing in spite of the rain. Jemma did not notice her mom; she was trying to remember the definition of metonymy, and was this what she was guilty of? She'd been to college, and more college, and could remember nothing. To know it is going to rain is one thing, to have a historically aberrant torrential downpour arrive following your wedding in the gap hours prior to your reception, and to think of aged relatives and already drunk friends making the drive to the desert hillside country club in a city without excellent drainage, is another. The other bride, Eliza, was asleep on the bed. Eliza might have been your guess to wear the tux, but, the couple was not conventional in their unconventionality, and both wore dresses.

The mother of bride one, Poll, was flitting from room to room at the Twin Arrows Navajo Casino Resort, popping her head into all the rooms on the reserved floors (of which there were two, seventy rooms in all) that responded to her hurried knocking and stating some form of: "Jemma is fine. She's known rain was a possibility for a long time. But we do think it best to limit the vehicles that make the drive over to the country club, so maybe try and pair up with the room next door? Or however you want to cluster?" More than the Rygaard half of the guests were familiar with Poll, her meddling was famous, and so the general understanding was, of the two moms, Poll was the controlling, pushy, locally powerful woman. She ran a library in suburban Milwaukee.

Room 334 held Joyce and Rick Mack. Joyce was a coworker of Poll's, and Rick the husband excited to be in Arizona for the first time. Even just a hotel, any decent hotel, was enough for Rick. Flagstaff might as well have been Aspen in his eyes. As the rain came down, Rick would stand post a couple times an hour under the large Twin Arrows entrance portico, smoking, and think, "Mountains!" He'd married Joyce in a church, her childhood church in Kenosha, and had never considered another venue seriously. The alternative, in his mind, had been Vegas. He said this to Joyce back in 334 before Poll knocked, and Joyce, thinking her man wonderful for announcing his thoughts as he did, told Rick, "No. You've created a false dichotomy." Rick nodded and Joyce silently questioned her understanding of the term she'd just used. Poll gave the Macks her update, apparently necessitated by the change, or arrival, of weather and Rick asked, "How's Eliza?"

Poll exhaled in the doorway. "Eliza's napping."

Rick had seen old, literally old, family friends of Eliza's checking into the room next to his and Joyce's. He went into the vacated hall after hearing Poll knock repeatedly next door, unsuccessfully, and head back up to her own floor. The Macks were the room second nearest the stairs, the elderly couple, the nearest. Rick rapped on their door softly and took a step back so he would be in full view for whoever was screening visitors, the man or the woman. The door opened and the old man, white v-neck undershirt, khakis hiked and belted, wearing a new looking Yankees cap, liver spotted arms, wet protruding lips said, "Is she gone?"

"She is," said Rick. "It's really raining. When my wife and I head to the reception, can we take you and your bride?"

The old man coughed and slowly turned his back completely to Rick to speak to his wife somewhere in the hotel room. His undershirt was tucked into his briefs. "Do we want a ride, Ruth?"

And Ruth shouted, "We do!"

Calls to the suite became frequent. Eliza was awake, naked on the bed, eating strawberry ice cream she'd ordered from room service. She felt joyous. She had a crazed smile on her face, and Pepto-Bismol colored ice cream remnants ringing her mouth. Eliza was a person who appeared most comfortable naked. Physically, Eliza belonged to the magnificently feral Fairuza Balk, PJ

78

Harvey breed of woman, though she didn't know it, and would not be particularly struck if the resemblances were pointed out to her. She did not want to ever talk about her appearance; which is different than saying she lacked confidence in her looks. You might have guessed her for a tux only because of a detached masculine assuredness she projected. Eliza answered the phone by saying her own name. A friend of Jemma's from college was asking why the casino's shuttle service couldn't be utilized in traveling to the reception. The friend on the phone kept saying, "Just might be easier's all." Eliza listened to Jemma's friend and watched the TV, a timber sports competition sponsored by a chainsaw manufacturer, and ate the last of her ice cream. The friend was still talking. Eliza said into the phone, "We have to go. Poll might know!" and hung up. She then picked up the phone and ordered another bowl of ice cream, "Yes, strawberry again, please." Jemma was lying next to Eliza on the bed, naked too, a bit in awe of this woman she'd married, as if Eliza was her own child, and glowing with the feeling that she'd married right.

Old Ruth decided, after remembering that her husband was not going to take off his hat, that she would wear jeans to the reception. She was in the shower at the time. She'd wear a blouse and blue jeans. It was settled. Their table would be in the back, away from first dances, speeches, toasts; it did not matter. Her husband had begun telling people he was hiding a surgery scar with the cap, then realized it was more effective if Ruth quietly gave away his invented excuse. It seemed completely true coming from Ruth. And she enjoyed lying for her husband.

Rick stood under the portico smoking, breathing in the West, thinking of movies he could rent from the library upon returning to Milwaukee that could sustain the feeling he was currently having. The last western he'd watched had been *Wyatt Earp*, loaned from the library maybe two years earlier, but he'd struggled with Costner. Costner was so clearly a successful businessman, a boat owner, a Parrothead, a man who spent money on watches, Rick didn't know if any of this was true, but nonetheless it made the movie seem like a sort of hobby fantasy that had been filmed. Rick knew John Wayne wouldn't do it for him either. Maybe no actor would. He wanted a western that was just the wooden towns, planks over puddles, the desert. Sustained shots of western frontier towns and the voids between from the POV of a horse. A horse being ridden by a benevolent cowboy, maybe not a cowboy at all, but some quietly persuasive salesman. Rick often had daydreams related to this one, usually while playing baseball or football video games. His desire was to be able to pause the action and with his character exit the playing field, get changed in the locker room, and walk around the city surrounding the stadium. The world outside the stadium would be paused too. A paused Kansas City in summer, walking out of Kauffman Stadium across the full parking lot into empty Arrowhead and its corridors, or walking out to I-70 and heading downtown slowly making his way between the cars. A paused frigid Green Bay in December, entering warm homes where the game he'd just vacated was stalled on the television mid-broadcast. Trying on a crew neck sweatshirt from a Green Bay closet. Opening a Green Bay fridge, then heading next door to do the same. Rick did not know what this line of thinking was about, but it was persistent in his head. It drew him back to these video games nightly. If he played long enough, he was able to project his paused-world fantasy and almost inhabit it as a reality before he snapped awake again. He tossed his cigarette and ran out from under the portico to get the car. The old man in the Yankees cap and his wife Ruth were standing with Joyce inside, behind elegantly tall sliding glass doors. Rick hadn't gotten the man's name. None of them had minded if he had a cigarette first; he'd asked. Ruth had said, "You're the one getting wet."

Poll was in the lobby watching the guests find other guests and make their way to vehicles. It was still pouring rain. She was aware of several people avoiding her, both with their eyes and their routes to the parking lot. A few couples took wild swings out to the perimeter of the lobby and skimmed along the wall as if on a ledge to get their cars, just to avoid her. She was not imagining things. Or, she was, but not these things. Poll was imagining a caterer

81

crying as Poll gave her welcome speech at the country club. A caterer who would go on to greater ventures. A caterer with a future. She imagined Jemma rolling her eyes at this caterer. Of the guests Poll observed heading to vehicles, it seemed the dress code had slackened in a way she found terribly upsetting. The rain had done this. The rain was in control. Poll was tired. She sat down in an overstuffed leather chair. There was a Native American pattern in the carpet. Poll had no way of knowing if the pattern was from the Navajo or Native American at all. She muttered, "Goddamn rain." She thought, "Sky is master," and then mouthed/breathed the words "Sky Master. Sky Master."

Jemma and Eliza saw Poll splayed in a sofa chair and walked across the lobby to her. Taking her mom by the hand, as if to rouse a daydreaming child, Jemma asked, smiling, "What did you just say?" Poll told her and Jemma asked, "What is a Sky Master©?" Poll shrugged and looked out at the rain. Poll was so tired, she looked like she might start crying. Jemma had been in this moment before and knew just to stay still. To wait for her mom's lull to pass. She knew this was coming, this lapse, and it would all be over soon.

Poll looked her daughter up and down from the chair; the fact of her daughter's adult size occurred to her, amazed her, caused her to shake her head. Poll kept shaking her head, and as she did the motion became separated from its awed origin. Poll said to her daughter,

"Please don't act like you know what's going to happen, or how it is that this feels."

One Dead, Sets Fire

A tornado had ripped through town followed shortly by volunteers. Students who were putting off college for a year or forever, idle believers, repentant businessmen, past and future rivals from the next town over, all showed for varying periods and intensities of work. Though "service" was the preferred term.

Will's house had gone untouched. It was summer break and he volunteered. He would not be going to college in the fall, but still regarded the summer as his "break." He'd never been outside of town for any significant amount of time, and to meet girls his own age from cities he'd never been to—from cities—renewed his interest in his own life. He'd been having regular sex with Erin Tackert, bony and slack, and increasingly Will felt she was a person to be escaped. Will had said nothing of her to his friends, sexual or damning or otherwise; their sex was known about and mentioned to him, and he would shrug in reply. What was there to be said? But he was still capable of cruelty in the usual ways. This was in Halesville, Illinois, two hours straight west of Chicago. In the fields.

National news coverage of the storm's aftermath lasted a single day. One elderly man had been killed. He'd been the only inhabitant of the town to not evacuate. One out of 570. He'd refused on some privately held principle. He'd started a fire inside his house shortly before he died using a squeeze can of lighter fluid and a large pile of his own clothes; this was observed live on television by a camera trained on the man through his back sliding glass door. The fence that would have prevented the view had already been knocked down. Once the flames were taller than the man, he took several steps back and stood very still. He stayed that way, rocking onto his heels, until the tornado reached his house. Most of the coverage speculated about the dead man's cause for starting the fire. A few townspeople very publicly respected his death for reasons difficult to explain or understand.

The news repeatedly played a clip of a defiant woman who looked like Estelle Getty from *Golden Girls*. She was sitting on the bottom of the two cement steps in front of her yellow clapboard house, the sky pooled dark above her, "You saw it?" she said. She was squinting up at a reporter, singling out the one who'd asked what she thought of the dead man's fire. "You saw it. Now what exactly would you say?"

Black haired, blue-eyed, freckled with a boy's name, the volunteer Will was consumed by was named Ryan. She was wealthy, round faced, had just finished her freshman year as a Literature major at the University of Chicago, and was fixated on the man who had died in the storm, Don Dryden. The first question Ryan had asked Will was if he had known Dryden, and the first lie he had told her was, "Sure, I knew Don."

No one in town knew Don in the way Ryan was asking about. From one day of tedious coverage a viewer could cull the following: Don Dryden had taken over the house on Porter Street with the brick chimney after his brother died and left it to him. Retired from a financial advising firm in Cleveland and moved to Halesville. The brothers had previously been estranged. Don was a harmless old bachelor recluse. He bought his groceries midweek early in the morning, did not get a paper delivered, attended no church, and kept a clean yard. He wore an Indians hat when he did his grocery shopping. The toothy grocery clerk had got a lot of airtime. And with that, any viewer would know as much as anyone in Halesville knew about Don Dryden. The viewer may or may not have realized Don's habits, or the lack thereof, had never been summarized and spoken and certainly not portrayed as dignified, until after his death.

Ryan got it in her head that it would be a good idea to reenact Dryden's final moments on a large scale. Her idea was to have fifty piles of clothing and fifty people holding squeeze cans of lighter fluid in a parking lot as the sun was setting. The people's movements would be coordinated like dance, the fires lit in unison, the slow retreat from the flames done together, the watchful stillness of the flames, en masse. Will started laughing, and then seeing Ryan's face, said, "I didn't realize—" He became serious about the piece instantly, and told her the only parking lot large enough would be in Morton Lake, at the Wal-Mart.

The Morton Lake Wal-Mart sat off the highway next to a deep swampy acreage of trees. Within this bog was the lake described in the town's name. It was not swimmable, boatable, constant, a lake, or easily reachable. Through the muck and dense undergrowth, it would be a clawing twenty-minute hike to the standing water. Lanky, bored Erin Tackert worked at the Wal-Mart. At the outer edges of its parking lot, backed into a space facing the miry forest was where she and Will had often had sex. On a Friday, weekend, or summer night shift, Erin would call home and say that her boss was offering overtime, it would be another hour, hour and a half, and Will would meet her near the trees, parking near the store's entrance and walking across the lot to her car, all alone and humming with the black woods rising behind.

Daytime, thick and buggy. Will took Ryan to scout the parking lot for her reenactment. He expected to see Erin in her blue vest and nametag, walking to her car for cigarettes, or eating a candy bar on the molded plastic bench provided for employees. She wasn't outside. Her car was. A ten-year-old white Subaru wagon in an alert stance.

"This will work," said Ryan. "Will it be obvious what we're doing, since we aren't going to be in Halesville?"

Will thought about how to answer. He was conscious of trying to flatten his initial emotional reaction. "I think it will be obvious that we are recreating Don's last moments. I don't think it will be obvious what we're doing."

Before Ryan could enter into what he'd said, Will asked, "Should we have the store behind us or the highway or the forest or the road in? Behind the reenactors, I mean. Behind all the fires, I mean."

"The forest. Most neutral solid background."

Since Will wasn't going to be caught by Erin Tackert in the parking lot, he decided to initiate contact. He asked Ryan, "Do you want something to drink?" She said she'd wait.

He didn't see her at any of the checkout lines, and didn't see her restocking any of the children's clothing near the front. The store smelled like stale microwave popcorn. He walked to the right and towards the back past the toys and bikes and nearer the sporting goods. He found her in a dim aisle with tennis rackets and junior golf sets, on a short ladder. She smiled when she saw him and he smiled back, forgetting his purpose. He thought about how she'd never made fun of him when he'd come quickly. Or when he'd been weak with tenderness in a way outside of how he wanted to be understood. How within the chances she'd had to cut him down or even take note of when he was exposed, she'd pretended there was no such opportunity. This moment in the feebly lit aspirational sport aisle was about sex, Will knew it. This girl, he thought, patient, but also without hope; this was his own construction. Will imagined she'd foreseen some end similar to the one about to happen. He was attempting to diminish his callousness. Erin had three older sisters still in town and had witnessed much worse, Will thought. She'd smiled when she saw him, but her smile had disappeared as soon as Will had returned it.

She came down off the ladder and walked up to Will, but didn't touch him. Erin crossed her arms and looked over Will's shoulder before looking him in the eye.

Will was mumbling quietly, realizing she already knew everything. "I didn't want to not tell you. I'm sorry."

Erin sighed. "It's been texts nonstop. Telling me they saw you with her. Since a week ago. So don't feel big here now. My sisters took my phone until I promised not to call you. I don't have your number anymore," she looked past him again. "She'll be gone soon too, you know."

"*I'm* going to be gone soon," said Will, fully sunk into the movie he was watching of his life. He was thinking about how Ryan had tied his hands behind his back with her socks. He'd snuck into her host family's house, an upper window tree reach, and she'd asked him to pretend his hands were still tied once her knot came loose. How she'd bit his earlobe hard, failing to draw blood, and said if he made any fucking noise she'd leave him bound. Leave him period. How she'd told him he was not and would never be in charge. He did not dispute this. He wished he could tell Erin about this girl's soft domineering. About how Ryan slept in socks. If for no other reason, because he knew Erin would laugh if these were events removed from her life and shown to her. If it were in a movie they'd watched mistakenly. Erin would have laughed at how hard Ryan was trying.

When Will walked back out to the car, Ryan was taking pictures of the parking lot and the forest beyond with her phone. She was struggling with the angle. She looked at Will, and before she could say anything he said, "When are we going to do this?"

Ryan's volunteer group's leadership found out and forbade its members to participate in her reenactment of Don Dryden's last moments. If any of their volunteers were discovered to have participated in such a reenactment, or any similar event, their college credit would be revoked entirely for the duration of their time in Halesville.

And so: it was six fires at sunrise. Ryan at the head of the pyramid, Will behind her, and the remaining mounds of burning sheets purchased from Goodwill occupied by two other strident U of C volunteers and the boys who wanted to bed them. There was no crowd, but Erin was there and her co-workers willing to walk outside, trailed by the assistant manager delegated to put an end to whatever was happening in the parking lot.

Ryan stepped back from her burning pile of sheets, and the two girls and their boys did the same, all watching her movements. Will watched Erin watching Ryan. He looked like a spaced out kid in a school play. Erin was smiling at all this effort. Will set down his can of lighter fluid and stepped completely away from the fire, dropped his Indians hat to the ground. He stood next to Erin. He watched the rest of the awful slow dancers, standers, as they stood post at half attention to their fires, saw them as Erin did. Will came up with something to say.

"When I die, I'm going to make sure to be alone. Out of view."

Erin, still enjoying the whole scene, reached out and took Will by the elbow, "We don't know any better than she does." She leveled her gaze at Will and then turned back to the show. The reenactment was deteriorating. None of the hats fit and the fires had grown threatening. Followed by no storm and no loss of life.

Insurance

I worked with Kuthan. His wife had kicked him out of their flat little house in Mesa. When I met him, those were the words he used to describe where he lived, "Flat little houses. The whole street's like that." I liked him instantly. He was short and laughed easily, had large sad brown eyes, and like everyone in Phoenix, was from somewhere else. The few natives of the Valley let you know their rank straightaway. But somewhere else, place, was not a part of Kuthan's self-identity. He lacked nostalgia for other cities he'd lived in; I admired this enormously. He was born in London, but from age ten had been raised in New Jersey. Then Michigan for college, Las Vegas, now Phoenix. Kuthan spoke without any traceable accent and had no apparent religion. He was an ideal suburban Westerner.

But now he was kicked out and Kuthan's understanding was that I was in a similar situation—I wasn't—and so he asked me if I would put him up for a few days while he looked for longer-term housing. This was a Friday, lunch hour. We were seated in the air-conditioning at a health focused sandwich spot across the burning street from our office building in Tempe. Our tan three-floor office building was in full view from the restaurant. Kuthan was eating a leafy salad full of bright slivers of carrot. "Office looks like a fat neighbor watching," he said, spearing the spinach with his fork.

"How'd it happen?" I asked.

"Her sister. She thinks I have something going with her sister."

"Younger or older?"

Kuthan set down his fork and made a sputtering sound with his lips. "Older," he said, "A lot older."

"How old are you?" I asked.

"Thirty-four," he said, plucking leaves of spinach out of his salad with his fingers.

"About what I thought. How old is sister?"

"Forty-nine."

"And is it true?"

"It was true once. A single time. In our laundry room off the garage. She put her sandals in the dryer for some knocking around noise. Left our house barefoot."

"That's how your wife found out?"

"No, there were no clues. She just ended up knowing."

Kuthan arrived at the condo at sunfall. I was living in Scottsdale, north of where we worked. The condo was in a gated community on a golf course, owned by my uncle who I paid rent to directly, in cash. Only fifteen of the seventy units were occupied year round. The development would be mostly empty until winter. It was where I had retreated. My uncle was thrilled to falsify a lease, underreport payments for tax purposes. This was a greener part of town. Weepy Native Willows, tall oaks, a few Palo Blancos chalky and reaching, richly dark oleander trees blooming coral, white, red, and palm trees everywhere. The foliage was stranger and more inclusive-making than any gate or slow-driving badge making the rounds. Three minutes into the dusty north would tell you that. Or the dusty west, east.

The "community" was surrounded by insurance company buildings, three story and tan like our own office in Tempe, but these all, conspicuously, had mirrored windows that doubled the pink dusk, the orange sunsets nightly. Kuthan had never seen anywhere I'd lived; I'd never been to his house in Mesa. We'd met up less than ten times outside of work, early on Saturdays, Sundays, to watch Chelsea matches. Kuthan was a Chelsea fan from childhood, seemingly the one marker of origin he did carry with him. I had and have no rooting interest, but was glad to watch these games. ESPN and the like marred most televised sports for me, all hagiography and marketing. This was more present in the E.P.L. than anywhere, but the most tabloid of the coverage still had not fully come overseas, and we told the bars we didn't need the audio, encouraging them to keep some other match's sound on. Kuthan didn't mind. Beer, silent soccer, certainly not traditional or particularly communal as that sport's viewing is so often celebrated, but for me, ideal. Other than those bar meetups, this was the first stretch of real time I'd spent with Kuthan.

He parked on my driveway, and I told him I was glad he did, because it was against the H.O.A. bylaws to park on the street. Kuthan asked me why I was whispering. He smiled holding his navy blue duffel as the sun dropped, and we both seemed to register the silence settling in full—looking to the tree branch shielded second floor decks, the stucco nooks and private walkways. Kuthan swatted a mosquito at his neck, and asked what flower it was he smelled. I told him I didn't know, and that it had taken me the whole of my month-long stay so far to learn the trees. Emerging from around a darkening bend, walking down the middle of the unmarked road, was a knobby-kneed old man in high khaki shorts and a red shirt that read "Satan Is Permanent" in white lettering. He wore a bucket hat pulled low, boxy blind-man sunglasses, and raised his hand in a prolonged greeting. His gait was arrogant. We raised our own hands in unison, and as the man passed, he said, "Welcome." When he was out of sight, Kuthan shouted, "SATAN IS PERMANENT," and I held out my arms meaning, shut the hell up. He did, then qualified his shout with, "What is it you think he wants us to learn wearing something like that?"

"Don't make mistakes," I said. "Satan is permanent."

"Like: don't fuck your wife's sister," Kuthan said. "Satan is permanent." Then he looked in the direction the man had been walking and added, "Or, we could take it as general encouragement to craft our own outfits."

My front door was on the side of the condo. Where the front door should have been, was my garage, and above the garage, the unit itself. We entered and walked up the broad dusky tile stairs to the unit. Kuthan remarked on the large mirrors, the high ceilings. Two bedroom, two bath.

Two white noise machines had been left behind, one on the granite kitchen counter next to the coffeemaker, and one in the master bedroom on the nightstand. My uncle had tried to dull any outdoor noise from entering. Car horns, knocks, bells—even distant—had caused his rescue terrier, Bernard, to go off barking. Such a machine seemed redundant in this place, like the gate. But, my uncle was doing me a favor and so I kept the machine in the kitchen running in memoriam of his goodwill, the absurdity of the setup, and as a reminder that the arrangement was temporary. Kuthan didn't seem to notice the purring machine's static emission. Instead, he went directly to the wall spanning built-in shelves filled with CDs in the living room, in the middle of which was a stereo. My uncle had, to Kuthan's delight, not saved or returned to his vinyl upbringing, nor dove into any of the streaming services.

"What's with the offices as I came in?" Kuthan asked as he walked the alphabetized shelves of discs. "Looked like it was all insurance."

"Couldn't tell you. One is a 24-hour call center," I said. "That's all I know."

"I thought those were overseas," said Kuthan.

I shrugged, "So did I." Kuthan was taking a great amount of pleasure in locating the speakers scattered in the upper reaches of the living room, looking over the stereo's buttons, adjusting faders, grinning as the CD tray emerged. He said, "I've been all Spotify for over a year now. This is like high school. A better setup, though." He delicately placed a disc on the tray, hit the button to close, then hit another button to skip ahead somewhere deep on the album. I heard a thin whirring as the CD player caught up. Then, the opening twelve-string strumming of "Sundown" by Gordon Lightfoot spilled down from the ceiling.

"This is one of those you have to play loud, or it's silly. But played loud you can start to understand why it's great."

"Why's that?" I asked. I had never witnessed someone taking Gordon Lightfoot seriously.

"It becomes hard to remember where the song began or how long it's been playing, what it's about, or what any of it has to do with sundown."

I didn't know what Kuthan meant. I didn't enjoy parsing lyrics and had never talked about volume as it related to influencing the quality of a piece of music. I said, "That's just the beginning of the thought, right? 'Sundown, you better take care...'" I almost had said, those are just words, right?

Kuthan watched me politely equivocate and he said, "I should've started with: When this song is played loud, I can get lost in it, and it works."

Thinking about it now, Kuthan may have refined his thoughts on the song within the unconscious suggestion from the lyric, "Getting lost in her lovin' is your first mistake." We started drinking beer, and Kuthan added to the list of songs he needed played loudly in order for them to take effect. He scanned the spines of the jewel cases and played exemplars as he discovered them: "Sing for Your Supper" and "Dedicated to the One I Love" by the Mamas and the Papas—thirty seconds into the latter, when the rest of the arrangement comes in on the turnaround, and the bass arrives climbing with the harmony vocals, and the whole song explodes, I had a brief sobbing fit, smiling, shaking my head, and Kuthan nodded his assent—then, "Let Me Roll It" by Paul McCartney, "Papa Hobo" by Paul Simon—it went on, Pauls and Papas, until "When You Were Mine" by Cyndi Lauper.

Kuthan was done choosing, he said so, and lay down on the couch, asking me to take over. He said he'd never heard a lot of the Dylan I was mentioning so I put on "Abandoned Love," "Pretty Saro," "Red River Shore," "Huck's Tune," we listened to all of *Planet Waves*, which I said was, if allowed the indulgence, my second favorite record from The Band. But Kuthan wasn't really tracking. We had overlap in the music that meant something to us, surely, but we hadn't been raised together, been in cars together at age seventeen, hadn't learned anything together about what we loved most, and so we put on TV, the end of a Grizzlies/Warriors playoff game in Oakland. The entire arena was yellow. Maybe he'd seen something in my face, how much his indifference to *Planet Waves*, specifically, had surprised me, because he asked, "Can your wife do Dylan?"

And because he was no longer just a person that I worked with, or that I occasionally had watched soccer with, I decided to answer honestly, in full. Or, full enough. "We aren't actually married. The ring was for when I started working in offices. All the way back doing temp work in Chicago. She preferred me to wear a wedding ring. She said a ring and my general demeanor would result in me being left alone."

"And without the ring, that demeanor draws women in?"

"The highest compliment she may have ever given me, never actually voiced."

Insurance

We were still drinking, maybe five beers in each. Kuthan had switched to bourbon and had set about trying to find the number for the call center located outside the gate. At some point, he'd walked his duffel into the guest room and gotten changed into Michigan basketball shorts and a gray undershirt. When he returned to the living room wearing this outfit, I understood we were going to be up for a while. Watching him drink in shorts reminded me of college. And like in college, we'd used beer, music, and televised sports as a panacea for talking. And thank God. When those routes fail, or dead end, there arises the need to venture out.

Kuthan was regarding me differently. Maybe waiting for me to tell the rest of my story. He appeared to be reconciling the man he had previously understood me to be with the one sitting in front of him. He seemed vaguely impressed. I caught this in glances. Why had I not ever told him I wasn't actually married? Had I thought so little of him? Truth was, I hadn't known it would ever matter. I still don't think it matters. Presenting technicalities and specifics: the exact age I'd moved somewhere, my legal marital status, the details seemed unnecessary. Or, the details could have been replaced by invented details, and had been, with the same result. But, I see now, I was the one who'd fessed up, who'd admitted the deception. Still, Kuthan should've understood, he'd moved all over and left people behind. What does it matter what his former co-workers, friends, knew or didn't know, *specifically*, about him? Their perceptions were not him regardless. Kuthan's own portion of withholding was not asking where my not-wife was, not asking what had happened.

The answer was, she hadn't gone anywhere. She'd stayed in our apartment in Phoenix. And I was still paying half the rent. The particulars of our trial separation were embarrassing to me. The fact that I had an uncle willing to provide me with discounted rent enabled our situation. Without him, we'd be broken up. Having to explain any of this to Kuthan would have necessitated me distinguishing our situations from one another. I wasn't confident I could do that as fully as I wanted.

Kuthan was having trouble figuring out online which of the insurance companies ran their call center from Scottsdale. He suggested we take a walk and see which of the buildings still had lights on, cars in the parking lot.

We walked past the mirrored buildings and were surprised to find most had underground parking garages with long sloping entrance ramps down, barred by metal roll cages. I'd never really noticed. Kuthan did not look the part of detective in his sleepwear, barefoot. He looked abandoned in this setting. The pattern of landscaping around the buildings was manicured grass, flowerbeds laced with a loose mesh of ruddy irrigation tubes, palm trees, and full, enormous oaks. At the base of the palms, small spotlights shot upward, dramatically shadowing the canopies. There was no humidity, no wind, no sound, except occasional birdsongs, both guttural and chirping. Complicating our search, nearly every building had lights burning on several levels. We walked over lawns up to various office windows for a better look and saw only empty cubicles. We continued walking down the street. Then, Kuthan said, "Over there, it must be," noting four cars parked side by side, above ground, and an entire first floor lit. "I see someone."

The building in question was occupied by Nationwide. Standing twenty yards away from the building, behind an oak trunk, Kuthan found the 24-hour number listed on their website. The first agent to pick up was in Pittsburgh. It was after three more calls, and an actual request to be transferred to someone in Scottsdale, that Kuthan succeeded. He motioned with me to walk nearer the window with him. Like a boy playing spy, he was crouched as he approached the glass. I followed, but kept my distance. He tripped on an irrigation line and went down, dirt caking his knees. I heard Kuthan invent a policy number as he stood, and then say, "I apologize, I must be looking at the wrong thing. It's a nine-digit number? Top right of the bill? Let me look. What city are you in? You're kidding. I don't know for how long now, my wife and I are splitting. I'm transferring. Currently waiting for re-assignment. No, makes it sound more serious than it is. You know what, I think maybe I can see you."

At that point I started backing away. I didn't want to be with Kuthan if security arrived, but I couldn't exactly leave him, at least not in any permanent sense. He was my guest regardless how this turned out. And he didn't have a plan. I was watching him make it up. He was a free man in so many terrible ways.

I heard him say, "Red shirt. Stand up. See me waving? You have no idea how hard it was to get to talk to you."

And I stayed very still, hiding back behind an oak. A cottontail darted across the street, and then another, maybe sensing we were endangering the immediate area. I was willing to stand against the tree until things quieted down. But Kuthan started shouting my name, first and last, over and over, and it became clear I wouldn't be able to hide much longer. Kuthan's chant became even more pointed and joyous, "SATAN IS PERMANENT, SATAN IS PERMANENT—" and I knew I wasn't hiding at all.

The next morning I had two messages on my phone, one from security and one from my uncle. I didn't bother to listen to either at the time, though the one from my uncle ended up being particularly heartening: "They can't tell you to leave. I own the place. Do whatever you want. For another month." I made coffee and took it outside, where I sat on the short slanted driveway next to Kuthan's car, looking at all the trees. Dumbfounded by all these trees in the desert. I didn't want to be inside when Kuthan woke up. And then, like a fable, the old man, the "Satan" man, was headed down the middle of the road again, but this morning his shirt was a deep green, and the lettering, I couldn't quite make it out. The letters were black. I squinted at the man, his shirt, but today he did not raise a hand in welcome, and his shirt, though I foolishly expected it to, gave me no answers. I like to think that it said, "Keep Moving."

Shelly

We were into eastern Colorado, into that flat, liminal region that could be misrecognized as any plains state, before we saw another gas station. The land was bleached, ascending. Desert hidden under burnt brush. The gas station had a green long-necked dinosaur out front, a more capable beacon against all that white than any sign. Shelly ran ahead to use the bathroom and I went through the aisles waiting. The gas station was understocked. Many of the bright candy bar cartons were empty. Rolos were all gone. When she found me, Shelly widened her eyes, meaning, "That's better," and started looking for a chocolate candy called a Blue Monday that she'd had once in Kentucky. She said the man she'd been engaged to was from Kentucky.

She looked tired, frowning at the low shelves, settled for an Oh Henry! and we got in line. Shelly was dressed like a marathoner. Black runner's tights and a zip-up windbreaker. It's embarrassing now, but I only noticed

Shelly's hand as she set down the chocolate. Her sutures were ink black, almost glossy, knotting the stub of her left ring finger. The finger was cut down to her first knuckle. Brutally. Like a gambling debt settled in a back room with a serrated blade. A raw pink ridge of flesh and clearly new. I have no idea what he normally saw come in off the highway, but the man behind the counter seemed to be registering Shelly's hand as I was: her punishment was too deliberate. As if she now carried a warning, marked in a way criminals mark other criminals. The man looked at me wanting an explanation. Shelly was searching her jacket with her good hand, doling out coins as she found them. She didn't acknowledge that the man's gaze kept returning to her left hand, which she kept flat on the counter. And she did not turn to me. Maybe she'd not wanted any of her stitches' stiff knotting to catch in her coat pockets and kept her hand out for that reason. And only now realized she was found out. Or maybe she'd chosen this moment for me to see what I should have already.

Shelly's missing finger gave her and me, us, a new weight; and it was *us*, the man could see that. He saw it before I did. I don't know where this specific thought came from, and it was solely a projection, but in that moment having a kid with Shelly occurred to me. Or, more specifically, her carrying my baby. I'm a little sickened by stating it that way. We'd never had sex. Came close, I think, but that was when we were nineteen or twenty, almost a decade ago by then. I hadn't even seen Shelly in close to six years. And she wasn't pregnant. But I felt that kind of love, expectant love, watching the man watch her; I felt that connected and protective even though I had no idea what had happened to her finger. Or why she hadn't told me, shown me, during the three hours we'd already spent in the car. Shelly smoothed out a balled up dollar next to the scattered change, using her good hand. The man behind the counter pushed his cap up on his forehead. "How much do you think a candy bar costs?"

"Oh," Shelly said.

"That's fine, just hold on to the bill. Always need change."

The man shifted his broad jaw into an exaggerated underbite, nodding as she pushed a few last coins across the counter. Again, his look went from her face to her hand to me for answers. Because we both knew, the man and me, she could have kept her hand hidden. She could have just kept it at her side. Or bandaged. If I could have spoken to the man without Shelly hearing, I would have said, "It's new to me too." The man spoke to Shelly but looked at me, "He making you pay your own way?" I smiled in spite of myself and we left, back on the highway.

We'd met in Hays, Kansas, at the college there, where we were both students. I was raised in Hays and for me Shelly might as well have been from Paris. She was from near Sterling, Colorado. Ghostly freckles and tawny brown hair, slightly bucked teeth. She had a way with a cigarette that was distinctly not from Kansas. Taller than me. Long limbed and completely inconsistent. There was one week straight we were at the Mall Cinema nightly, re-seeing *Lost Highway*. It only ran a week in Hays. A mix-up with a print of *Rosewood* brought it to us. Shelly would unbundle from her coat and watch with her mouth open. And the next week, she'd say movies are not made, but instead "generated, systematically." I had some idea of what she meant. Then it'd be listening to Rachmaninoff laying flat on the floor in my dorm. Her room was never offered. As if going there was consummation. In my dorm swinging and swaying to the second piano concerto. Then Dinosaur Jr., the Carter Family, Linda Ronstadt's first few solo records, and Leonard Cohen, especially *Death of a Ladies' Man*. That's just a few. All offered up and later discounted by Shelly. Dinosaur Jr. and the Carter Family: "One note." Ronstadt: "Early on, she's entirely lesser covers." *Death of a Ladies' Man*: "A musician's most accessible work should probably be discounted." I don't know where she got the things she said. Her opinions always felt to me like re-stated sermons. And in that way, she seemed distanced from her choices, like, I later found out, a lot of sad people do.

Shelly

It was a night relationship. Relationship is the wrong word, but so is affair, bond, link, even friendship's wrong; the most truthful way to put it is just to say it was a night thing. Wet summer lawns and blurry walks and meals in a packed glowing Waffle House in the middle of dark Kansas. Jostling for a table. Students everywhere. Options were limited. Head on the table drunk. And I'd miss class the next morning. Shelly would not. Most of our time together was drunken and small and trivial. Drunken for me, small and trivial for her, is how it felt. She told me so once, in those words. But then she'd be outside my dorm the next night waiting on a bench, as if we'd made plans. It's dumbfounding to think about, looking back, because we were in Hays, Kansas, and where else did Shelly have to be? Nothing was going on, but it always seemed she could have been somewhere else. That she had options for how she spent her nights, but had relented and chosen me. I'd walk anywhere to meet her, beg a car off my brother to take her somewhere, whatever it took. She seemed to be coming quietly undone in a way that allowed me to know her as I did. That was my thinking. A gap in her judgment allowed me to be in her life. Childhood's a gap like this, a long suspension of thought where neighbors are friends without cause, and loneliness is a gap like this too.

Maybe it had been a year I'd known Shelly, or it was in that first year, and I was at my brother's house asking his car off him for the night. They had a little square pre-fab home. Their front door opened directly onto the lawn. My brother had his wife in a headlock in the middle of their yellow kitchen. His wife was bent over like some animal, her face turning red from strain and laughing. She looked right at me from within his hold. My brother let her go and they both straightened themselves out, my brother cracking his neck and looking to the ceiling and his wife punched him in the chest. My brother staggered, smiling, and gave me a wild look, "That's why I married her!" he said. They acted like this in their house. My brother's wife started making a peanut butter and jelly sandwich and my brother sat down at the kitchen table. I remember my brother wasn't wearing a shirt.

"Do you not see what's happening with this girl?" he said.

"No, tell him like you told me," his wife said.

My brother understood what his wife was driving at, but said nothing. He waited for his wife to say what he knew she would now inevitably bring into the open.

"You're a placeholder," she said to me, finishing the sandwich next to the sink. She looked over her shoulder, watching me not comprehend.

"What're you saying?" I asked.

"She's using you. She is." She licked the dull knife clean of jelly.

My brother's wife set half the sandwich on the table in front of him and they both chewed, watching me. Mouth full, his wife added, "This girl might not know it. She might not realize she's using you. But that's what it is. Ask her why she doesn't drive her own car?"

My brother cut her off, "Enough, enough."

I had no response. I recognized that what my sister-in-law was saying was true, instantly, but could not account for how it could be so. Or, couldn't account for how I didn't already know. Shelly must have had a car. She was from out-of-state. I didn't see her for days at a time. Where could she go on foot to escape anyone in Hays for more than a string of hours? But I'd never seen any car. There were questions I was unable to ask Shelly. Out of fear. Fear of no longer being allowed her presence. Those were the terms I thought of her in. I was young. Young, young, young. Stupidly and persistently.

All of it is stuck in my head chiefly because of the knife, watching my sister-in-law lick that knife. It was the most sexual gesture she'd ever made, would ever make, while holding eye contact with me. She's years since divorced from my brother and it's still the memory of her that I have. And I remember getting the keys off the hook below the phone and leaving their kitchen clearly knowing, I didn't care if I was being used.

I didn't end up finishing school. I left midway through junior year. A decision I stand by. My brother and his then-wife left town and bought a Tex-Mex restaurant in Lawrence and I went with to assistant manage. I'm still there. Full manager. Shelly began dating an older man, men, at some point before I left school. Or she had been all along. I never got the details. I didn't know other people who knew Shelly. I didn't have anyone to help answer the questions I had about her. She graduated with a nursing degree and stayed on at HaysMed, the hospital. At some point in the last few years she found me online. We talked a bit on there. Vague and flirtatious. I was guarded with her; I tried to be. Seeing pictures of her on my computer had a dulling effect on my memory. Peering over her coffee mug in her blue scrubs. Her responses would come immediately or not at all. I was going to be in Hays with my brother for a couple days, sleeping in our parents' house, looking at two spots where we were thinking of opening another restaurant. Smaller, just tacos, aimed at students. We knew the locations, had our whole lives, but my brother was set on standing on the land before beginning any conversations with the owners. I clicked through enough, too many, pictures of Shelly and let her know I'd be in town with some time. She called and asked if I could take an extra day and drive her back to Sterling. Her parents were selling her childhood home and she wanted to see it before it was sold. The house was already empty.

"Do you have a car?" I asked.

"Of course."

"Did you have a car when we were in college?"

She started laughing. "Yes. You always wanted to pick me up. I kept it with William. William who owned the record store."

I'd known William in the way you might know a certain tree in a neighbor's yard. There were only two places to buy music other than the mall. William was a rail thin, generally unimpressed man with a dyed black mustache, and dyed slicked hair. I didn't know Shelly had ever spoken to the man. We'd bought records in his store together without acknowledging him. Without making eye contact. "Why can't you drive yourself?"

"I'm embarrassed to say."

"Car sick?"

"Well. I could make that part of it somehow."

We squinted merging back onto the long straight stretch of highway. "Why'd you wait three hours before showing me your—" my voice trailed off, unable to settle on a noun, not wanting to seem upset. Another question came, "Were you really engaged?"

She was staring straight ahead, her mouth held as if she was about to speak, a hand on each knee. I groped for the sun visor. The day was burning white. Even the concrete road itself was a shade lighter since we had crossed the state line from Kansas. The road and the sky were both so washed out there was no boundary between them.

"It was never about 'showing.' You weren't looking for it. It's easy to hide when it's not being looked for."

"If you're going to lie why ask me to be here?"

"Because I can't grip the wheel."

She held up her hand and I looked at it expecting to find it was somehow faked. But it wasn't. I looked hard at her hand and then hard at the road. The fact that Shelly was missing a finger somehow validated my memory of her younger self.

"I lost it three weeks ago. Working retail."

It took her a while to speak again, and it came haltingly, but she gave me the story. She said she had worn her engagement ring to work. That she had been engaged to a man from Kentucky. That she had worked at a Target, not at the hospital anymore, at a Target. The hours had been getting to her at the hospital, overnight, and switching to days wasn't an option. The Target job was temporary, an in-between, she'd been ashamed and didn't tell me. She was on a ladder in the back. She said her job was pulling and stocking items. And reaching out, stretching away from her footing on a ladder, she slipped. On her way down her ring caught in a notch in the shelving and ripped her finger off.

I didn't know how to process or move past any of what Shelly had said. I felt I couldn't turn the car around when we were a half hour away from Sterling. I tried to let her story dissipate.

"Is highway blindness a thing? Like snow blindness?" I asked. The road and the salt stained land rushed to meet us. Blurring, burnished.

"It's not the highway that's blinding. It's the sky. We're closer to the sun, where I'm from," she said.

"How long until we see mountains?"

"We won't," Shelly said. "We aren't seeing any mountains."

I took this to mean I misunderstood where we were headed and what I had agreed to do and it must have shown on my face because she said, "We'll be there before we get far enough west to see the mountains is all." Stretching everywhere were white fields, heat rising and folding into the sky.

"Tell me about Target," I said.

Shelly closed her eyes, maybe to remember, "It smells somewhere between a new car and a dog."

I pulled to the side of the highway. A maroon sedan I had passed in the left lane twice, and a similarly familiar yellow and blue truck shot by. Then a string of three white cars.

"Everything you said happened, happened?"

She reached out and held my wrist with her mauled hand, "You think I did this to myself?"

"Of course not," I said, shaking my head. I hadn't thought she'd cut off her own finger. But now I did. Felt that way with certainty. But why? And why would she do it? I'd agreed to drive her before knowing about her finger, hadn't I?

"I want to talk to the man you were engaged to," I said. I wanted confirmation that some piece of what I had been told was true. She was still holding my wrist.

Shelly reached into the bag at her feet and handed me her phone, saying his name, "Brian Luther." I scrolled through her contacts to L, found his number and dialed. I held the phone up to my ear and as I did, Shelly began speaking at me, describing Brian Luther.

"Nearly has a unibrow but he's so handsome in the face that it doesn't matter. Wide, squarish hands. Strong. He's a contractor. Works for his father—"

Brian picked up the phone and said, "Shelly? Are you ok?" I could tell he was outside.

"Sorry. Brian Luther, this is a friend of Shelly's. Sorry. I'm realizing how crazy this sounds? You were engaged? She told me this story about how you two were engaged and her finger—"

"Are you with Shelly?" Brian Luther asked.

I told him I was. Shelly continued talking the whole time. She was telling about how they'd met, Brian Luther's sister was a nurse at HaysMed, he'd been visiting, he wore boots, didn't own sneakers. A police car pulled to the side of the road twenty yards ahead and a cop got out and began walking towards us.

"If you're with her now, then look at her fucking hand," Brian Luther said.

The cop knocked at my window. Made a motion with his hand that I've seen understood as "yeah, yeah, yeah" or "roll down the window." Shelly kept detailing Brian Luther: Doesn't drink, doesn't go to church. Coffee with lunch, coffee with dinner.

"I'm not there for a reason. You did this to yourself," Brian Luther said. He hung up.

The cop knocked much harder, with his whole fist. He yelled. Shelly said, "He's going to say if this isn't an emergency we can't stop here."

A Father's Story

My son came into my office and handed me the assignment from his second grade teacher, written on a half-sheet. He was wearing sweatpants and had his T-shirt on his head, draped back over his shoulders, so that he looked vaguely like a pharaoh.

Parents, please get online with your child and help her or him find pictures of what she or he thinks the future will look like. Please send the pictures to our class email address for presentation tomorrow.

My son linked his arm with mine, standing at my elbow, both of us looking at the blinking cursor waiting for our search.

"You know what you want to do?" I asked.

"I've seen the future," he said.

"Where?"

"Grandpa showed me the future on his website."

I didn't know my son had seen my dad's website. My dad had created an online memorial for the Air Force base he'd been stationed on in Montana as a young man. The base was long defunct and now in ruins. His years in the military were his golden few, years I believe he had forgotten and recast as idyllic by reducing them to the only two stories he told: How he played cards on his bunk with the sleepwalker Eddie Vargas, and how on the nights that my dad won big, Vargas would lurch around violently, muttering my dad's name, until one of the Airmen, one of the awakened crowd in boxers, punched him in his gut. The other story involved a freckled farm girl and a kitchen table, and a father who emptily promised he'd shoot to kill; though my dad says he did limp for a period of months. Strange that both of these stories are night stories.

My dad traveled to the base over fifty years after he'd been stationed there and found what looked like the remains of a P.O.W. camp stripped of its barbed wire fence.

We pulled up the site. On my dad's website there were pictures of him standing matter-of-factly on the cement foundation of the barracks he'd lived in, of him pointing to the remaining section of a skeletal radio tower, maybe thirty such pictures in all; and he put these pictures side by side with old black and whites of the same places from when the buildings still stood, filled with life.

"That's the past," I told my son. "All that's the past."

My son was not swayed. He tapped the peopled black and whites on the screen and their desolate color counterparts fifty years advanced, "Past. Future. I'll say what Grandpa said."

Initially, it had only been one kid who got upset. Just one boy. Something about an old man standing alone in empty Montana had scared him. I understand this fear. In the photographs my dad is bent, set starkly against an enormous sky. I can see how a boy might think, "Who left that man out there? How did he get home?" Maybe this boy could imagine my dad shuffling away from the tripod to beat the camera's timer, how often he was too slow to get positioned before the shutter clicked. The pictures with only the photographer's long shadow in the foreground were especially frightening, I was told. My son repeating, "Here is my past; here is my future," couldn't have helped. One kid getting upset led to the whole class getting upset. Upset in the second grade means crying. At first my son searched his classmates' faces for support, "That's the future," he said. He didn't understand how it was possible to deny what was plainly true. I was told he grew defiant; crossing and uncrossing his arms at the front of the room, restive with the scene he'd created. Someone called out, "These pictures can't be the future, the future hasn't happened yet." My son wouldn't sit down. He wore a look that dared anyone to confront him directly.

Checkup

I agreed to meet my stepsister, Sarah, for breakfast. She picked an early hour, early enough to make me think she'd turned some corner. That the late night phone calls from Van Nuys, from addresses I could usually hear being painstakingly slurred to her, that those phone calls had stopped. She's twenty-three, ten years younger than I am, and didn't become my sister until I was around her age.

Sarah was already seated in a corner booth by the window at seven, her back to the door. Watching the waves of morning traffic queue up to get on the 405. Traveling deeper into the haze. The rest of the view was flagged car dealerships, power lines, and twinned restaurants. Slim clusters of palm trees. And a looming rectangle of a hotel that set the parking lot in shadow by proximity. This was a place I'd never been. It had the bones of a Denny's, but was called something else. Colored differently. Pinks and blues. The air conditioning was louder than the music. Some sad Clapton record was being droned out. There were muffled kitchen sounds, then clanging, and I caught the eye of a short Latino cook through a long service window behind the counter. He ducked back to work. An unshaven, dog faced man stepped in close behind me gripping a newspaper. Red plaid shirt and nearly white jeans, breathing heavily. He scanned the empty restaurant, saw my sister, and went to the opposite corner, growling, "Crowd."

Sarah's green scoop neck dress and gray cardigan were pressed-looking, and I tried to understand what this meant about her living situation. What could have changed in two weeks? On the phone she'd said she met someone, but I hadn't pushed her for details. Two weeks earlier I'd picked her up in the middle of the night. She was standing in the front grass of a dark low-slung bungalow. A shoddy house in between tidier identical models. She wore no shoes and a short, flouncy skirt. She got in the car and tucked her wet feet underneath her, directed me to the Motel 6 where she was staying in a practiced, oddly syllabic way, nodding. There were specks of grass down her legs. I told her $70 a night was not something she could afford for any length of time. That I couldn't afford it. She nodded more quickly and ran her tongue along her front teeth. She said, "This is night one, don't fear," and gave me an addled salute. She was living out of her suitcase, clothes rumpled and scattered, her two best outfits draped over the backs of chairs on separate sides of the motel room. The outfits she would use to try to once again be a dental hygienist. Her toiletries, including the motel soap bar and motel toothpaste had been lined up on the edge of the TV stand, mimicking targets at a shooting gallery. So, her hand had been recently steady. That was my takeaway. I'd only caught a glimpse of the room through the door. And I didn't ask her anything. Because I knew everything comes out eventually whether you like it or not.

She was drinking water without ice, and cut her eyes at her purse as I sat down. There was still no waiter to be seen. Sarah's face was scrubbed, a bit of mascara, clean brown hair to her shoulders. She self-consciously took a deep breath before looking at me directly. The green dress was one of her over-the-chair outfits. The rest of her clothes, those not in her suitcase or strewn, were in a storage locker I was paying for.

"Did you ask for it that way?" I said, meaning the water.

"I did. But I smiled first and said 'Good morning.'"

"Where is he? I saw a scared cook. And that guy, reader, over there."

"He'll come by. We call 'reader,' 'Nolte.'"

My view was of the whole restaurant. Our corner was cold, stuck beneath a vent with blue transparent streamers dangling. A tall German looking waiter came out of the kitchen wearing an apron. He half pointed at me and half at the ceiling, meaning he'd be a second, and sat down at a table covered with open salt and pepper shakers. As he filled the shakers, he'd bring two to eye level and clink them together. A flurry of car horns erupted outside. I kept watching the waiter, and Sarah turned in her seat.

"That's him," she said.

"Who's 'we' call him 'Nolte'?"

The German looking waiter saw I was staring and mimed pouring coffee. He was ten feet away. I said, "Yes, coffee." And Nolte shouted, as if it was a soldier's name, "Coffee!"

"That's him," Sarah said again. "That's the man I met."

"The German waiter is 'we'?"

"Luuk. Dutch waiter. Luuk," she said, reaching out to clutch Luuk's forearm as he approached.

Luuk turned our mugs over, smiling, and poured us both a cup. He set the coffee pot on a table behind him and stuck out his hand for me to shake. His friendly hand swallowed mine.

"Hi, hi. Nice to meet you," he said, in an accent I wouldn't have been able to place.

I excused myself as Luuk set down menus and I went into the bathroom to wash my hands, take a moment. Objectively speaking, I knew more about Luuk than any of her other past "boyfriends." I knew he was employed, and where, and his name. I knew that he saw her in the daytime. I rubbed water on my face, under my eyes, and then felt ridiculous for doing so. The music in the bathroom was different than in the dining area, it wasn't music at all, but a hushed Spanish language version of public talk radio. I dried my face thoroughly and checked my collar for signs of wetness. When I came back Luuk was seated next to Sarah in the booth, taking a drink of her water.

"You don't do ice either, Luuk?" I asked.

"Bad for your teeth. Chewing the ice is bad for you," he said, grinning. "Sarah taught me that."

"You must learn fast. Just don't chew it, right? Don't you want cold water?"

He stood up, "I know myself. If I have the ice cup, boy, I'll chew it. So, I avoid it, yeah? Sarah said you like eggs medium-rye-hashbrowns?"

I made a face and thanked him. I was uncomfortable with being charmed so easily.

Sarah had been watching me intently during my interaction with Luuk. Her new man. The polite empty banter, her general quiet, all was to show me progress; it was possible the two could have rehearsed some of what had just happened. Which was fine. If he was willing to help her, that was something. But Sarah did not trust easily, and withholding was unlike her.

"You're living with him?" I asked. She was drinking her coffee like a woman in a commercial. Two handed, her fingers interlaced around the mug. She set down the coffee and pushed it near the napkin dispenser.

"I'm staying with him. We cleaned out a little closet he doesn't use."

"So you'd like your stuff from the storage unit. How big is the apartment?"

"Three bedrooms. It's here in Van Nuys, or, actually—" she turned to find Luuk, who was speaking to the Latino cook through the service window, "Is your place, is it technically Panorama City?"

Luuk knit his eyebrows and said, "Yes," before it seemed he realized what Sarah was asking.

I asked Sarah, "There's a roommate?" before Luuk said "Oh, *my* place," out loud to himself behind the counter.

"I haven't met the roommate yet. He's away on business," then preempting my question, "I don't know what he does. Travels a lot. He's Dutch too."

She nodded, as if to emphasize she was telling the truth, as if to agree with herself and coax herself to keep talking, and Luuk was back with more coffee. He was more handsome than most of the wait staff I'd seen at diners. He had a long nose and wide mouth. And did not appear to be in any hurry.

"Sarah said you're teaching in Tujunga. And live there?"

"Both, Luuk. Living and teaching."

He stood for a moment, grinning. "Great," he said, before walking over to fill Nolte's cup, which Nolte had been holding in the air above his head for half a minute.

"Where'd you meet him?"

Sarah's elbows were on the table, and she opened both her hands palm to the ceiling to indicate the restaurant.

I took my key ring out of my pocket and removed the small key for the storage locker, sliding it across to her. I'd held on to the key to prevent her from selling her belongings. I believed it was my only tether. "I pay it on the 5th. It's $80 monthly, if you end up keeping it."

"You're thinking I'll end up needing to keep it?" Sarah said.

"Do you still have a little money?"

Sarah nodded, dropping her eyes in a way that made me think she did not. I almost asked about her car, if it was running OK, but I'd seen it in the lot, which was a sufficient answer. When Sarah had moved to LA I'd made her promise to call me for rides on nights that she was stranded. Seeing her gray ninety-nine Taurus, my old car, as I arrived for breakfast allayed some of my fear, which was day-to-day. Seeing her car meant that at least for the previous night into this morning, she'd made choices with consequences she could handle herself.

Our food came and my plate was heaped with a double portion of hashbrowns. Luuk also brought a side plate of six sausage links that we hadn't ordered. Sarah was laughing as I picked up a link, "If you eat that, it means you approve."

The food, just it arriving, had settled her. "Luuk's a provider," Sarah said. I kept my head down through that comment, halving a sausage with my fork, quartering, and chose to not ask what she meant. It sounded too much like a lifted line, a post-coital reassurance, too much a part of the life she'd been having trouble recognizing for what it was. Or the life I'd hoped was over.

She'd been a dental hygienist for a year, north of San Francisco in Larkspur, a monied, quaint, and self-nostalgic town. A job that her stepdad, my dad, had arranged through an old college friend, a dentist. The story I'd been told was that she hadn't gotten along with the other hygienists, all of whom were much older, entrenched, and that Sarah had left on her own. My dad had said something like, "Sarah wasn't welcomed in the way I'd hoped." But we both knew that was, at best, a lie we could tell each other over the phone. That she'd probably just stopped showing up, or come in nodding and half put together. As far as I knew, she was still licensed, nothing had lapsed or been revoked in the past several months since she moved to LA. But tests had never been the problem.

The first time I met Sarah was at a restaurant in LA. The hostess was my age, black skirted and stockings, leading me to the table in a way that made it difficult for me not to watch her lower half. So, I felt uneasy and handled from the start. Other than the hostess, there were a lot of non-wives. The men mostly seemed to be my dad's age. Off work, bloated. At the time, Sarah and her mom were living with my dad in his apartment in San Francisco for the six months leading up to the wedding. It's strange to put it as I did, that I "met" Sarah before we were made family, but it's the case. She was long necked and slouched at thirteen, and alone at the table when I arrived. I was in my first year of graduate school in LA, and the three of them had taken the slow Amtrak south, twelve hours, for the weekend. Sarah was third wheel, unwillingly and consciously, on a trip resembling a trial honeymoon. Sarah was alone at the table when the hostess left me, slowly tearing a napkin down its center. I told her who I was, putting my hand to my chest with misguided earnestness and I remember asking where my dad and her mom were, and she shrugged. There was a beat, like that beat of uncertainty sometimes felt on a blind date, after the blind is first lifted. I'd not known many only children. Then, the first two things Sarah said to me were, "How many of you are there?" And I told her about my two older sisters, married, back east, and Sarah said, "How does it feel to be my brother?"

The Latino cook came out from the kitchen, seemingly dazed, and Sarah called him over, introducing him as Manny. And up close, I no longer had any sense of him being Latino. He was a tan white, weathered beyond his years, maybe Japanese, or some hardy combination. We thanked him for the meal, and he gave us a thumbs up as he walked backwards towards the door, "Going for a cigarette. Possibly several." Through the front window, I watched Manny plant himself in profile, lighting up something that was clearly not a cigarette. Even from that distance, he was conscious of me watching him and gave me the same thumbs up he had thirty seconds earlier, now with the glass between us. He put his head back to laugh, take in the sky and exhale.

I asked Sarah where Manny was from. "Here. He hides himself well until he speaks. And he's white. He hides that too."

We finished eating and I asked Sarah why she'd dressed up for breakfast with me, why the outfit. "This isn't for you. I have an interview at nine-thirty," she said, dabbing the corner of her mouth.

It was though, the outfit, the effort, however brief, small, it was for me. Even the fact that she'd mentioned an interview. Luuk, too, was a showpiece. We'd met for meals in the past few months, or, really, I'd paid for her to eat. But she'd never been on time and never this put-together. She knew I'd offer up the key when she gave me any semblance of a plan, and it was her token of success, of trust. She knew I was ready to be unburdened. But Sarah never would have called and simply asked for the key. She wanted to show me she was fine. That she was ready to resume a type of life, with monthly bills and flat dailiness.

Checkup

She stood and brushed off her lap, saw I wanted to hear more and said, "It's in Encino if I get it, ok?" She smiled, beautifully.

I paid Luuk at the counter and Sarah gave him a small kiss, leaning quickly into the register, smacking her elbow. She shook her arm loosely at her side as she went to wait out front. Manny was still out there, now actually smoking cigarettes. Nolte whistled and barked once, empty mug held above his head. I went to the bathroom.

Luuk came in and was at the next urinal. He asked if I had liked the sausage, a question that, due to his accent and my unwillingness to make eye contact in the moment, I had trouble parsing for intended irony. I told the tiled wall, I did, and thank you. There was one sink, so Luuk demonstratively let me wash my hands first and after he was done I asked him to hold on a minute. He straightened, and his whole demeanor became expectant, the friendly glibness gone.

Before I could ask him to put my number in his phone, in case anything happened to Sarah, or if she left to call me, or, really, for *when* something happened to Sarah, *when* she left, before any of that, Luuk stopped me. In a flat American voice he said, "Wait, wait."

But I didn't wait. I caught the word "misunderstanding," and that was enough. I was trying to stop Luuk, or Luke or whoever he was from explaining himself as I left the bathroom. Sarah and Manny weren't out front. I could hear Manny chopping up hashbrowns on the griddle. Luke was shaking his head trying to communicate something to Manny, who was watching us through the service window. Manny ducked when I turned. I told Luke to stop.

"Who are you?"

"Luke, I'm Luke. I'm an actor."

"You don't work here? You're not a waiter?"

"No, no. I am a waiter, I do work here, I'm just also—"

"Is Sarah really staying with you?"

"She stayed with me last night. It's a misunderstanding. She asked me if I could do Dutch. If I wanted to try out a character—"

I waved my hand for him to stop and stepped out front of the restaurant, dialing Sarah's phone. Traffic was still gridlocked, stammering to the entrance ramp. It went to voicemail, her phone was turned off, or dead. I felt I'd know everything in a few hours, days at most, that I could go and wait at the storage locker for her to collect her belongings. But I also didn't know what that would accomplish. What manipulation had she been willing to endure in order to enact her own? That was the question that kept returning. I didn't know then that she was gone. Nolte walked by, newspaper tucked under his arm, holding a full mug of coffee from inside. Stopping every few yards to take a sip. I walked back into the restaurant. Manny and Luke were standing in the center of the dining area, looking up at a rattling air vent, then stared at me, puzzled.

"Do you know if she really has an interview?"

Their expressions only changed in recognition that I had spoken. Still, I'd asked for a reason. I didn't want anyone, strangers especially, to know I'd given up on her.

How I Got This Job

My brother, Sanch, addresses a long table of his co-workers in the corner of a low-lit steakhouse near closing. Sanch is standing and swearing joyfully. He smiles for punctuation. The reaction he gets is favorable, but still mixed, which he doesn't notice. I usually call my brother something else, his name, but I've solely heard him called Sanch here at this long crowded table. His nickname only seems invented because you haven't met his co-workers. Collectively, their tone and rate of opinion delivery are combative, hateable actually, if you are not among them. Brashly raising his voice one man admits without any detectable provocation that he pays monthly for porn; he gives a dollar amount that I believe is a lie, maybe quadruple the real figure. I think: *Subscription.* The monthly man texts another man at the table a link and then watches for a reaction, but the man receives no text and says, "You must have sent it to the wrong person." And it's not so much that this man is paying for porn, or accepting an exorbitant auto-renewal charge for content he could get for free, but instead that he waited until his wife passed out drunk, two chairs away, to begin talking at all.

Some of the wait staff is watching our table from across the room, trying to be seen enough to encourage us all to leave. Leaning around corners in white shirts. I tried to beg off having to come to this thing, but Sanch, it's infectious calling him that, gave me a spare key to his apartment and told me to leave the dinner whenever I wanted, knowing I'd end up staying. Free meal and all.

I'm in Chicago, staying with my brother for a few months until I can find somewhere to live. He makes more money in a year than I'll ever hope to make in four-years-work, and is charging me nothing for rent. He has not brought it up, money, and shakes his head whenever I do. Sanch is my younger brother. His beard is fuller than mine, he's more handsome than I am, but I am much taller. All of Sanch's close friends are women, despite what this dinner might project, and he sees an astounding number of first run major motion pictures in the theater. Five a month, easily, he told me. I didn't and won't ask him this question, but learning these aspects of his adult life over the course of our first days living together since boyhood I think, *Is Little Sanch OK?*

This is a going-away party for a man that everyone at the table, except me, has worked with very closely for the past three years. The man is going through a divorce and is very friendly. The kind of friendly that, when he saw me enter, he said to Sanch, "That your brother? He sits next to me." So here I am sitting next to him. Thankfully though, the others at the table have monopolized his attention. He is changing careers, moving, and thinking of going back to school, this friendly man losing his wife in his mid-thirties, and many at the table are attempting to discourage him from school while trying to stay cheerful. The efforts of the anti-school faction are increasingly pointed.

A heavy man in heavy glasses leads the charge: "Stay with what you know, which is not school, *not* school and— shit have you read that new, new-ish, *Mother Jones* on effective altruism? I mean that's the key for you—not paying for more school, Jesus, I—"

This heavy man seems to be on the margins of his own thoughts. I enjoy being adjacent to the attacks against the almost-divorcé's plans.

The bald man on the other side of me can't stop talking about cars. "Perfected technology" is the term he keeps using. He puts his hand up, miming the motion of adjusting a rearview mirror. The bald man says "Perfected technology. When you adjust a rearview mirror, even minutely, it sticks, it's perfect, it's perfected. Cars are full of perfected technologies; it's why we are all so safe now. Automatic braking will be standard in no time and then we won't even be driving. That's what I want to do, I want to find more gaps that need perfected technology. Like when I turn on my computer I want to know how many emails I have, all my alerts all my notifications, I want that right away, I don't want to have to click into three different websites, I want it all on one page. I want to know—"

I stop him. "Doesn't that already exist? That must exist?"

He says, "And maybe it does. But I don't know about it, and that's part of my point."

It seems he could fold anything I could possibly say into his "point." As he continues listing the small technological achievements that proliferate inside what he is calling the "common modern sedan," I find "Doesn't that already exist?" a powerful conversational tool. It allows me to project interest and ask a question without knowing anything. And it is malleable: "That name sounds familiar," representing essentially the same tactical approach.

The bald man goes on, "Car cigarette lighters. Perfected, yes, but obsolete nonetheless, although not a victim of *planned* obsolescence—"

Anyway—a week later this bald man drives to Indiana, purchases a shotgun and blows the back of his skull across his living room and into the kitchen, where it slides down the polished surface of his refrigerator like a wide wet slug. His sister, a somewhat well-known city blogger, writes an article on the heels of his death about how she understands the suicide. Her author photograph looms enormous at the top of her posts, the site's choice, of course, but still regrettable. The sister looks like a hedge fund manager's carefully chosen fiancée.

Her interpretation, paraphrased, is as follows: There are options available to the man that wants to kill himself. Pills, razor, car, heights—my brother chose a gun. And there are options available to the man that wants a gun. My brother chose to obtain his gun in the way most Chicagoans who kill choose to get their guns. Not in the way most Chicagoans buy guns, but in the way most Chicagoans who *kill* buy guns. His death is not social commentary, but my interpretation is: if we want to kill in this city we know how.

Her piece in full is not stat-heavy but includes a link to an article that states, "60 percent of the guns recovered at crime scenes in the city between 2009 and 2013 were first purchased outside of Illinois. Each state in the country contributed at least one gun used in a Chicago crime—nearly 20 percent came from Indiana…"

I read Sanch the piece out loud in his quiet spacious apartment. The most we hear in this building is a dog being shushed in the hall late on a weekend afternoon. We never know why the dog is shushed, or even if it's a dog, because we've never heard barking. The voice just seems like a voice aimed at a dog. Sanch does not have an immediate reaction to the piece. He makes me show him the author photograph again. He says the photograph makes him think of brunch. Her white collared shirt and ponytail. I tell him that kind of reaction might mean he hates women. He ignores me. We agree she has equated gun "crime" with gun "deaths" in places, problematically. And I tell Sanch I find her emphasis on "choice" and "options" strange when talking about her own brother's suicide. I tell him I would struggle with those words if I were in her place. "But still," he says, "the criticism has surpassed the art in this case."

I tell him within that statement suicide is the "art."

"Poor word choice," he says. "Poor choices all around."

Assuming the bald man's job requires very little training. I try to keep my memory of him alive throughout these early days in his cubicle by remembering our time together, saying aloud a third variation of the construction he helped me to understand: "That sounds familiar, tell me your approach though." I look my trainer full in the eye and say this. And when I have enough money from the job the dead bald man has helped me to obtain, I hope to further honor his memory by noting all the small miracles in the car I plan on buying. All the advances that I'm truly not even supposed to notice, all the little perfections humming, trying to keep me alive, on-time, awake, employed, warm.

Fuller

Fuller was having a run of bad luck. That's what I could glean. I didn't know Fuller, wouldn't recognize him on the street, or anywhere, and had never heard my brother, Jon, speak his name. But now Jon was talking about him a lot; my brother's half of the conversation seemed to be entirely a measured defense of this man Fuller.

It was after midnight, and my brother was on his phone in his kitchen speaking to another highway patrolman. The whole house was dark. My infant nephew had stopped crying from the back bedroom, his mom no longer cooing in Spanish. Still, Jon spoke quietly. It was a small house. I was flat on my back on the new kitchen floor we'd put in earlier. We'd nearly finished. Interlocking vinyl planks resembling wood, "Old Hickory-Nutmeg." There was a real novelty to lying on the floor in a house, in a kitchen. My apartment's long-rented, worn linoleum back in Chicago was not for laying down.

My brother was in a wide stance looking out the window above the kitchen sink as he talked on the phone. He was looking out over his little fenced-in backyard. Earlier that day, Jon had called his yard, and all those neighboring, "Home Depot yards," and initially that had made a kind of sense to me on its own. This part of Denver, which was not Denver, but its sprawl, was dense with new houses. Mazelike from above. That was my connection to Home Depot: density and shine, shelves full. Impermanence. But my brother then added, speaking more directly, that the fences and child's swings and deck sealant that made up the yards, that were part of the neighborhood's surface, had all been purchased from the store. He said that by "Home Depot" he meant Lowe's too. I was lost on what his larger point might be. Jon seemed aware of his non-choices as choices. That his appearance was no different than any of his neighbors', or fellow patrolmen's, struck me as emblematic of many of his decisions. A conscious and wary assimilator. Or so I thought. But Fuller, it seemed to me from the floor, made decisions that were decidedly not of a piece with the majority of those employed by the Colorado State Patrol.

Jon's responses that formed Fuller: "I'm telling you I had the conversation with him and used the words I'm using now: You can't see her. Can't drive past her house, can't go to her grocery store,"—"The year? Those headlights came in, maybe, three years ago, kind of ride on the side of the head, know what—right, right. It's a 2010 or 2011. Right. Ten or eleven Dakota. Right. Red Dodge. Maroon. That's him."

"Maroon" made me laugh. Jon said it slowly, fumbling with its roundness. My brother turned and looked at me, made a face that was an imitation of a disapproving father. Our disapproving father: a soft frown punctuated by a sharp turn of the head. From Jon, after not seeing him in however long it had been, a year? Year, little less. From Jon the frown seemed a small acknowledgment that he had been playing the role of a highway patrolman reluctant to offer up the word "maroon." I don't know if this was the role he played while actually on the job, or if he felt he was playing a role at all. Heightening his cop traits for my benefit. And I'm not sure if he was consciously mimicking Dad. I can't remember ever seeing my dad making faces in a dark kitchen.

I stood to share Jon's view. The land dipped and spread beyond the yard. The night itself was full of light. Shining solid walls and far-off nestled glowing pockets. It seemed hundreds of houses, in all directions, had motion triggered security bulbs, and there was the yellow summer moon. In the distance on a crest the glow of the highway could be seen. From the kitchen we could see a stretch of the highway's tall orange sodium lights. An oblong orange blur. Below was the hot white illumination of safety lights, stalled trucks, work.

Our father had a line about highway construction, when we'd slow to a halt and take in the men in their Day-Glo vests and stickered helmets. To not complain, that we must not complain was implied, well understood, and did not need repeating, but because we were still boys and did not know about money or how to earn it he would say for us, "Jobs. That's what being stopped here means." We lived in California as boys and California is nothing if not highways, so we heard about jobs a lot.

My brother arched his back, his feet set far apart, and from the bedroom the baby was wailing. Jon mouthed, "Hold on," to me without lowering the phone from his ear. There appeared to be long gaps in the conversation he was having with the other patrolman. Jon was waiting as much as listening. His eyes darted around the kitchen. It seemed some approval was being cleared. The baby kept crying. Jon walked gently through the living room and said something to his wife in the bedroom. He came back into the kitchen, stepping over the portion of flooring we had yet to complete. Due to my own mismeasurement we'd left a hand-sized rectangle of exposed subflooring. Noise-wise, too late to fix. Jon nodded back into his conversation, said, "I'll get over there," into the phone as goodbye and what seemed a tacit promise to keep whoever he had been talking to updated on Fuller.

Jon's police cruiser was parked on a slant in the driveway next to his wife's Honda Accord. I couldn't see any neighbors on the street or in house windows, though several were lit on an upper floor. In second story windows: warm light on vacant ceilings and emanations of blue TV; neighbors were awake. It was the hour of true crime murder shows, *The First 48, Deadly Women, Forensic Files.* The cruiser made me think of TV murder, had me scanning windows, projecting viewership.

"Is Fuller going to be in a cop car?" I asked.

"He hasn't been with us a year, so he doesn't get a take-home cruiser yet," Jon said. "Maroon meant his truck." He paused, looking at me. "I thought you were listening."

We got in the Accord headed towards E-470. Jon shut off the E.S.L. program his wife, Lupe, listened to while she drove, and asked that I put on some music from my phone. J.J. Cale had just died so I put on *Naturally,* skipping to the third song, "Don't Go to Strangers." We passed a grocery store with a huge empty lot, a Costco that lay on the fringes of an upscale outdoor shopping center, one of the largest high schools in the state, silent and mall-like, and several expansive, sloping, bunched neighborhoods similar to Jon's.

"She doesn't need those tapes," Jon said. "Tapes. Whatever they are. Downloaded. I don't know. She's accent conscious. Cleaning up the accent a bit," he turned to me, "I want her to fail."

"Say her name for me," I said.

My brother swallowed, maybe to dampen his tongue, "Lupe," he said, with a practiced, subtle accent. Like a Latino newscaster.

"I believe it," I said.

Ostensibly, I was in town to buy a car. That had been Jon's pitch after I told him I was in the market. My brother knew cars, said, get a one-way, I'll help you find a car, you drive home. Call it a vacation. I had all of July free and didn't have to be back to plan for the school year until mid-August. I had thoughts of heading out to California from Denver for something I was working on, considering working on, wanting to know if any of my memories of where we grew up still referred to a physical reality. An essay, photographs. Maybe only photographs. I'd need a camera. Denver felt so similar to where we grew up though, at least in its sprawl, I was thinking I might not have to leave. That my memories of California in the nineties could be accurately checked against present day Denver. It was a thought. But also I was in town to meet my nephew, see my sister-in-law for the third time and attempt to help out with the new house. Or, at least these were the reasons Jon piled on after I seemed to waver on traveling so far to buy what would surely be a used car. My brother did not need my help. He believed *I* needed *his* help. The woman I'd moved to Chicago to be with, and had lived with off and mostly on for a decade, had split. My days had lost routine and I'd lost all the assurance embedded in having my expectations met, even in disappointment. In our years together, she'd traveled back to California for my dad's funeral with me, had been to Jon's wedding, and had at various times spoken with several levels of my family intimately. I did not know where she was. Her leaving was long coming and already felt not of my life by the time I told Jon. I'll admit I'd hoped Jon would offer guidance with the car. Not knowing cars was a problem I could fess to, a problem I could accept help from Jon with, and that alone seemed reason enough to buy one.

We merged onto the orange-lit E-470. All the highway lights were new, so their pattern, a repeated round aura on the road itself, was unbroken. We passed a large pea-green billboard advertising a planned community, a whole new invented town, "Ridgelands," in tan letters. Jon said, "Eddie Bauer," paused, and said, "Separately, Menard's." We slowed at the brightly lit construction. A man in a hardhat stood with a stop sign held staff-like. Jon said, "Home Depot. Lowe's. Menard's."

I shook my head a little, trying to indicate I didn't need the Chicagoland hardware store equivalent offered up as further clarification. I counted four dump trucks on site, only one of which was in motion, rumbling loudly across the fresh gray lanes where we were stopped. The whine of a portable generator could be heard. Thrumming in swells. We smelled burning tar through the car windows. The construction worker holding the stop sign appeared to be staring at Jon. The man's gaze was not menacing, but was gaining darkness as it was sustained. The man staring with the stop sign was smoking, never removing the cigarette from his mouth, exhaling through his nose in distinct streams.

"I forgot you did that," I said.

"What's that?"

"Continue conversations like that."

"Like a horse, this guy, right?" Jon said. "Smoking like that? Out the nose is like a horse."

A saw started, sparks shot up from the highway and its whirring deepened, deadened as the blade sunk into the road. It was after 1 a.m. The banks of safety lights gave the scene the feel of an outdoor movie set-up. There were maybe twenty more construction workers than seemed necessary. "This light is dental. Dentist pulling the lamp down close," I said.

"Not paid like dentists," Jon said.

The smoking construction worker waved us on. I squinted at the stickers on his helmet as we passed. Squinted into the safety lights. Broncos. Holographic jaguar. Black lightning bolt. Muddled forearm tattoos. The man let his cigarette drop from his mouth.

"Fuller's new to the district," Jon said. "In Colorado, troopers have to live within thirty minutes of their Troop

Office, which usually translates to living within your assigned district, or the one adjacent."

"What district are we in? Are you in?"

"1B. Metro. Probably the most desirable for troopers with families. Best schools. Fuller wanted a family. I think kids was the plan with this woman."

"What's Boulder?"

"6C. That's desirable too. For some. For you maybe."

My brother went on to tell me about the first conversation he had with Fuller. Jon had been asked by his lieutenant to take a drive out to Limon, in the eastern plains, to the District 3 Post there, where Fuller had been working. Fuller had requested a transfer to 1B that had been approved, but included with his transfer was the slippery note that Fuller was "competent minded, able-bodied, loyal, and not for everybody." My brother was sent to parse this sentence.

"Limon might as well be Kansas. So I get to the Limon Post, which is just a collection of rooms housed within the Limon Town Hall. Fuller is waiting out front of Town Hall for me in a long kind of overcoat, well, kind of like you'd drape on a quarterback in cold? It's April. Mid-forties. And he's got these skinny legs. Bow-legged. Handsome. Hair looks wet. Short, combed. So he comes over and we talk as I get out of my cruiser. Someone had alerted him to the situation, maybe his captain who threw him under the bus with the note. So he's in uniform, but that's underneath this full-length black shell, and he's wearing it unbuttoned, as if he might shed it. Like some kind of Unitas. After the routine introductions, I mean right after, Fuller asks if I'd be interested in reading his screenplay."

Here my brother looked at me, maybe because I'd scoffed and maybe because he'd read some of my own attempts at the same. Fledgling, completed, failed. Hearing that someone else my brother knew, a highway patrolman, was more or less pursuing the same path I was, or had been, embarrassed me in a way I still can't completely account for.

"I told him, sure, I'd read it. And as soon as I agreed, he told me, well, don't worry about it. Then he asked if I had a pen, jotted down some notes on a pad. He said, if any of this interests you, I'll let you read it, because then I won't be exactly wasting your time."

"What did it say?" I asked.

"Open the glove box, it's still in there."

I read: —Blue paper cup of coffee —Bus travel —Woman without brother, father, boyfriend or ex-boyfriend. Possibly without sister. —Red leather jacket —1970s, but *BEFORE* 1977.

"And so I read that, told him I was interested. And I drove back to Denver and gave my approval on the transfer."

"Why'd you do that?"

"Whatever told Fuller he could ask me if I'd be interested in reading his screenplay, that instinct, that's useful."

We saw Fuller first in silhouette, standing in front of his small truck looking towards the wide front windows of the grocery store. The employees could be seen stocking shelves, carting boxes with dollies, resetting displays. A female manager was darting around supervising and briefly pitching in with various tasks. Fluffing bags of chips, pointing. She was doing a lot of talking with her hands. Everyone in the store was dressed similarly, dark green or navy crew neck sweatshirts, jeans. The employees were clustered in twos and threes, and young.

Fuller was maybe twenty yards from the store, his car parked facing the windows. The lot was dark, lit only by the ambient glow from the street and the store itself. Fuller was standing, rocking, his eyes trained on the woman inside giving orders. "That's his ex-wife," Jon told me, referring to the manager. We rolled up near Fuller's truck and when Fuller recognized the car, he walked over, quickly, as if Jon's appearance might be coincidence. He leaned down into the car and shook my brother's hand at something of an awkward angle.

"Listen, this is my brother and he was interested in maybe taking a look at your truck like I was telling you. If it's still for sale," Jon said.

"Did she call the cops?" Fuller asked, pointing at the store with his arm out straight. He was smiling as if he had just asked a different question.

"The call got routed to Don and Don called me. And I told him I'd make sure you got out of here. So if you are interested in standing around in grocery store parking lots, let's make it a different one."

Fuller stood tall and looked towards his ex-wife in the store. He spit somewhat dramatically. I laughed. He leaned back down into the driver side window, "I wouldn't sell you anything."

Fuller stalked off to his truck. Jon looked at me, "Don't laugh too hard."

I watched Jon get in Fuller's truck. Fuller leaned into his horn while protesting Jon's further involvement. All the employees near the front of the grocery store turned and looked at the parking lot, except Fuller's ex-wife. She kept on working, clapping to regain the attention of her staff.

It was a warm night. I reclined and started the Cale record from the top, had my eyes closed for half the first song when the music stopped because my phone was ringing. It was Jon. I sat up and looked across to Fuller's truck, watching Jon mouth the words I was hearing from the phone.

"Two things. One: I have to get home now, because baby needs diapers. Lupe called. Two: He's had more to drink than I thought. You need to come drive Fuller's truck to the house."

Jon took my phone, plugged in his home address and the phone announced I was about to make a twenty-five minute drive in current traffic. Fuller was rubbing his eyes with his fists. There were empty cans at his feet. The smell in Fuller's truck was of stale beer and a sickly vanilla, though I could not locate the source of the latter.

"I'll probably still beat you there. If not, wait to go inside. And Ben?"

"What?" I said.

"Thanks," Jon said.

"Yes, thanks, Ben," Fuller said.

Fuller wasn't acting drunk. We drove with the windows down and no music. I was driving just under the speed limit on the highway. The city and the black mountains were to our right, way off. Fuller's arms were crossed and he was sighing at regular intervals, turning to me several times to speak before he actually did. "Are you married, Ben?" he asked. He was almost shouting.

"Not married. The woman in the grocery store, that's your ex?"

Fuller sighed largely, "Since you potentially have the mistake in front of you, my story may have utility," he said.

"I was headed home from Casper, Wyoming, sitting in their airport. Natrona County. The woman you saw giving orders, she's from there. We wanted kids, had been married a couple years. Casper was on the short list of places she was willing to move. I kept telling her that's not a move, that's a return. Anyway. I fly to Casper, by myself, to see the town, see the department. Was there one day, a single day, and was headed home early because I knew pretty quick I wasn't going to live in Casper. So I'm waiting for my flight back to Denver that I paid extra to switch, a day early, and the young airline agent at the gate is putting on black cat ears. It's Halloween morning. She's adjusting the headband, chin down. Brown hair bobbed. Holding a little mirror she's darkening the tip of her nose, three lines on each cheek. I'm staring, realize I am, and look out the windows that open up to the airfield. My plane is sitting there parked at the glass."

I shot Fuller a look. He couldn't have known with any certainty my brother told me he wrote a screenplay, or *screenplays* for all I knew, but my thought was he probably wouldn't be telling his breakup this way if he did. Why'd I think that? Fuller was telling a story, was invested in the telling, and had an audience, me, that he probably felt had little to no expectations. Maybe my brother had told him I did a little writing, maybe not. Fuller was a drunk off-duty highway patrolman with an ex-wife. That was what should have been my surface understanding. And he was shouting the whole thing. But, I preferred being yelled at to having the windows up. He went on.

"I look back to her. The black cat is smiling. I turn, make eye contact with an old man who gives me a bemused 'all yours' kind of look before whispering something to his wife. The wife has defiantly long hair. Silver, straight, pooling in her lap. When I next catch the man's eye, both he and his wife nod in the agent's direction. The man's fidgeting around, laughing and blinking hard at his wife, leaning away from her. It seems he has trouble seeing her up close. The man's rubbing his white crew cut with these meaty hands. Has four turquoise rings on."

"Fuller," I said, and he turned. "What's the utility of knowing how many rings Grandpa's wearing?"

Fuller smiled as if my question had given us camaraderie, kept his arms crossed, and continued.

"So I get on the plane. Seats sixty-five. I'm midway back. My head's down while everyone's boarding, getting settled, and the black cat gets on. This seems like flagrant disobedience. Complete disregard for the rules of air travel. Rules I don't know, but her presence on the plane, in partial costume, just felt anarchic somehow. I watch. Her manner is professional. The black cat is confirming some passenger tally with the flight attendant, no rules are being broken. But I was shaken by her appearance. I take my phone, hold it up over the seat in front of me, zoom in on the black cat and take the picture."

He uncrossed his arms and jostled the beer cans with his feet, stuck a hand out the window. Waving his fingers as we went down the highway.

"And?" I asked.

"You're a writer, you pay attention, you can guess. The picture was found. And it sprung something loose between us. Why didn't I want to move to Casper? Why was I so fixated on costuming in the bedroom? Why was a grown man still stunned stupid by Catwoman? All fair questions from my wife. And the answer to all of them, and others: because I didn't want to be with her."

"So the message is, be with someone you want to be with."

"No message. But the utility of the story might be: marry a woman from a city you wouldn't mind living in. Desires for return are common. And hope that the city she's from is not tiny. In the bigger cities, wonderful Catwoman get-ups are not commonly seen on airport employees. Even on Halloween. I fell prey to a rural peculiarity. For the best, sure. Still, expensive, all said and done. Divorces."

Fuller slept on the couch I had planned on occupying and I took a sleeping bag to the kitchen and laid out on the floor. Lupe was not awake to protest.

In the morning, she stood at Jon's shoulder rocking the baby, watching him fry plantains in the method she'd taught him. Vegetable oil in a skillet, flipping the plantains as they caramelized. Jon had already scrambled the eggs and warmed a can of refried beans. To approximate the crema she'd had growing up, Lupe would take sour cream and add a quarter cup of heavy whipping cream, a little salt. The result was milder and richer than the sour cream I was familiar with. Jon was setting the fried plantains on a paper towel and heating thick tortillas on another skillet. Fuller had taken a shower and was in borrowed clothes, quiet. He seemed somewhat taken aback at the seriousness with which Jon was undertaking all this minor cooking.

We ate. Fuller was encouraged to serve himself first, and to not wait, start eating. He put eggs, beans, and plantains in a tortilla and spooned crema over top. Hot sauce too. He ate as quickly as a man who had made the meal for himself. He ate standing as the rest of us came to the table.

"Are you from Honduras?" Lupe asked, and in a coincidence of timing, the baby turned and looked at Fuller.

"Florida, Washington State," Fuller said. "What happened there with the floor?" he said, pointing at the unfinished section.

"It was my mistake," Jon said. "Measurement is not my strong suit."

This was not everything. And Jon's words did not allay my baseless heartache at having been replaced, but, certainly, for Fuller to be in this house was not bad luck. That run was over. I'd had that part wrong. Jon and I walked him out to his truck after we were all done eating. The sun was high and burning. Garage doors were open. There were boys on bikes shooting down the middle of the street in a V formation. Fuller's borrowed T-shirt was an XL giveaway, a faded Vinny Castilla. He was so clearly a man without a family. Fuller looked my brother in the eye and said thank you with the kind of finality that stood in for a promise. Then he looked at me and said, "Kelley Blue Book is going to be north of thirteen. I can do eleven."

A loose routine in a warm climate: heavy-pedaled bicycle for the chalky white sidewalk as broad as a street. Or it is a street, but without cars. There are vendors, but not densely. A woman with her hair wrapped up in a bandana tied at the crown of her head. *Women*, actually. All the women have their hair held in this fashion. There is a bar but I do not make it and I let nobody down. No one is waiting there for me. If I have a job I don't know what it is and I have not been for a long time. I have no memory of any boss, what her name might be or how she communicated disappointment or love when she remembered balance. No, now I am nightly sitting with a book and making notes on other paper. Notes about connections and listing words I don't know and when I finish with the book I start another and months later I can't recollect anything past and I have to start all over again, returning to some book, making new notes. There are no old notes. Old notes refer to nothing, their meaning never was. It would be against the days I've been having here to speak of old notes any more than I already have.

The world will end on a warm night. Muggy, buzzing dark in Chicago. Or in the deepest breathing forest in Honduras. In both places we will wipe sweat from our arms. Feel sweat down our legs and think nothing. We will hallucinate blinking radio towers and stumble towards the red round lights. Blinking. And then we will stop running. Panting in the crumbly black field or at the coast, the deserted hazed coast, the ocean grown newly terrifying. I will try and remember names but they will elude me. Instead: the quarter slots on the washing machine, the slam and chug with the heel of my hand, the care with which I placed my jeans and gray undershirts, inside out. The world will end on a warm night.

Rhymes with Feral

It is two in the morning on my Friday, which is Tuesday, and in the house across the street, lights are getting flipped off and on in a disoriented march towards darkness. I'm watching the scene from my window with a ginger ale, wide-awake. I've already had my allotment of three domestic light beers for the night and have switched to the carbonated without regret. The home across the street belongs to but is not occupied by Terrell Presley. Standing in the middle of the street that separates our houses, in the rocky desert hills where we live, I asked him a while back one burning, ticking day if the light switches in his house were placed oddly, if there had been miswiring, because this stunted fluttering with the lights always happens with his renters, and he, not unkindly, ignored the question. The creasing around his eyes deepened and he half smiled beyond me, as if a person we both liked was arriving. I want to be able to elegantly ignore questions without malice or consequence. But I really was curious about the switches, all the lights blinking. I've never been in the house and can only guess at causation.

Terrell takes extravagant quarterly golf trips with men he's known since boyhood. Men he grew up with just outside of Pittsburgh. Right now he's in Scotland. Last year was Brazil, at a resort where mostly undressed women offered kebabs mid-course. He told me cryptically: "I did not partake." Terrell has never been married, and in general, despite what his golf trips and the details he allows me to know might lead you to believe, is discreet.

I like Terrell because he is self-made and direct, even at his most opaque. He invented a surgical adhesive technology, sold it, and retired. He drives the same car he did pre-retirement, a pristine old Saab. He has always, until now, made a point to tell me a little about the person or people who will be renting, and reminds me to not hesitate to call the resort or him directly if there are any problems. I work from home, remotely doing IT consulting, and in all cases deal with his renters in a more concrete way than he ever does. Past renters have included an ancient couple from Ames, Iowa; a retired military chaplain; Terrell's dim and gawking sister. I've helped kill a snake, jump-started a car, and, by telephone, recommended restaurants, doctors, the most affordable liquor stores. My phone number is the only other contact Terrell lists on the fridge, I've been told. He knows I like to talk and don't mind questions from strangers.

Terrell doesn't seem interested to know my impressions of his renters. I usually open on his terms, asking, "Did the check clear?" But I wasn't able to do this with his sister, feeling it would be an overstep, so I had conspicuously little to say regarding his only kin. I couldn't reconcile her plain yokel qualities with Terrell's daily crispness. Of his sister, I only asked why she drove such an enormous truck, a Ford F-350. He told me he didn't know, but said, "Without the truck, would you have asked anything about her?" before heading back inside with his hands in his pockets. It occurred to me Terrell had bought his sister the truck. Maybe to give her some mystery. I have no proof.

Invariably, we have our talks in the middle of the cambered desert-worn street sloping between our two houses. The asphalt has been baked gray and is flecked by shimmering divots. We live north of Phoenix in Cave Creek, a place people travel to for their own golf vacations, which is the reason Terrell usually has no trouble filling the house in his absence. I've been told he could charge double his price. Our part of the desert is craggy and undulating. We have flat red peaks. Tan and pink bluffs, guajillo, Mexican Blue Palm, adobe houses tucked behind dog-leg driveways. I've found houses in Cave Creek to often be secretly opulent or secretly run-down. It's not exactly that all the houses look the same from the street, but instead that their flatness and positioning give away nothing. Landscaping is camouflage here. Locals take pride in the brutality of the summers, but I say any weather great masses of people over age ninety choose to be alive in, is weaker than advertised. Nothing like the Midwestern crush and tumult of winter, the sickening cold. And, here, if things do get too bad, San Diego is a five-hour drive, Flagstaff only two. As far as the renters that stay in his house, Terrell doesn't need the money, but something about his general practicality must prevent him from letting his house sit empty when it could be generating profit.

I'm at the window watching his house, now steadily dark, considering what has changed between Terrell and me. He'd said Scotland, offered the information freely, and when I asked about renters, was told there would be none. So, who the fuck is over there?

I slept late. It's nearly ten. I call Terrell's house, to see if the unregistered stranger will pick up—but the phone rings and rings. I walk into the kitchen and begin making something to eat. I put coffee on. I take out a non-stick skillet, spray it with olive oil, mix five eggs in a metal bowl, dump them in the skillet, now hot, and add a handful of shredded sharp cheddar cheese. I take out a can of black beans and microwave the beans in a Pyrex bowl. I take out tortillas from the fridge. I continue cooking the eggs as the coffeemaker sputters its completion. I have no idea how anyone makes scrambled eggs. I've been doing it this way for ten years now because I can't remember how my wife did it. My phone rings. The caller ID reads: TERRELL PRESLEY-HOME.

I say, "Yes, hello, this is Russ."

"You just called?" a woman's voice says.

"Yes, I did. Terrell usually lets me know when he has a renter, and so I was just calling to make sure everything is OK."

"If I'm not supposed to be here how would calling the house help?"

"I don't know how to—are you supposed to be there?"

"Yeah. Terrell is supposed to be here too, I'm not renting. I'm a friend."

"It's pronounced 'tehr-ull.' Like feral." What kind of friend would mispronounce his name? He's a Terrell like Terrell Owens, not Terrell Davis.

"I've never said it out loud," the stranger says.

I don't know what to make of this. "Well when does he get back from Scotland?"

The woman laughs, "I have no idea why he would have told you he was in Scotland. He's in Taos. He was supposed to be back yesterday before I arrived, but there was trouble with the plane."

I hang up with the woman and call Terrell. He answers on the first ring and I ask if he knows there is a woman at his house, he says he knows, that everything is fine, and thank you. He says he should be back tomorrow. I can tell he's ready to hang up, but before he does, I ask, "Why doesn't she know how to pronounce your name?"

"I believe in the past she's always said 'Mr. Presley.' Been in rooms with me where that was the norm," and then he does hang up.

He didn't sound surprised or annoyed. He sounded like he always does, calm and already mentally occupied with other concerns. I put the phone down, spend a few minutes finishing the eggs, and my doorbell rings.

Standing at my front door is a thick-eyebrowed woman in workout clothes. Behind her, on the street she crossed to reach my home, heat is rising off the asphalt in blurring waves. She's wearing earbuds attached to a phone she has in an inside pocket of her open zip-up. Under the zip-up she is wearing a white sports bra. She's young. Maybe thirty, and seems unaffected by the heat. Her dark hair is in a ponytail.

"I figured if I introduced myself, you'd see everything is OK. I'm Terrell's friend, Jordan."

I step aside so she can come into the house, say "Sure, sure," in sincere welcome, and we shake hands. Shaking hands with a beautiful woman usually makes me think of one of two scenarios: 1. If the handshake is strong, her father. 2. If the handshake is weak, her single working mother, and the apartment she'd had to herself, the thousands of hours of TV. I know this is fantasy, but, still, it remains. Jordan's was strong. Her loving father might have had no hands for all I know. No arms. The thought passes. To aid my unvoiced apology for the suspicions I earlier perpetrated on the phone, I ask Jordan if she wants any eggs, she says, "Sure, please," and I am more surprised by this than anything she has so far told me today. She is still wearing the headphones. The presence of another person in my kitchen makes me aware of its particulars: the size of the island suggesting a level of cooking I can't fulfill, the decorative copper roosters my wife loved still hanging, its dated brightness and comfortable femininity. Jordan sits at the island as if she was a regular customer. Her attention is not diverted by any interest in scrutinizing my home; she seems already familiar, or, possibly closer to the truth, unimpressed.

"Do you always keep those in?" I ask, pointing at my own ears. I'm standing against the cabinets in the corner of the kitchen, intent on appearing as non-threatening as I am.

"You're the second person to say that to me today. Well, not quite. The guy at the grocery store asked me what I was listening to, and I lied to him. I told him, 'Richard and Linda Thompson,' thinking that would stop the conversation. I was wrong. The kid lit up. He went on about how he felt they 'got in their own way a lot,' but when they didn't they were 'really magic.' He cited 'I

Want to See the Bright Lights Tonight' and 'A Heart Needs a Home' as evidence."

I make a face at Jordan. I haven't listened to or talked about Richard and Linda Thompson with anyone in twenty years, longer than that. By the way she was talking, even if she wasn't listening to Richard and Linda Thompson, she is making it clear she is familiar with their work. She seems dressed the wrong way to be saying the things she's saying, and too young, but this is a simple dumbass thought I try to get rid of. And I don't really know what the grocer meant. "What *were* you listening to?" I ask, getting her eggs situated on a tortilla I'd microwaved, scooping black beans overtop.

"Nothing. I walk around with headphones in so people won't bother me, but it hasn't been working since I got here." She tells me she is from Toronto. She watches me construct her breakfast without comment, sarcastic or otherwise, which is touching, and thanks me as I set the plate in front of her. She takes out her headphones, picks up the taco, and eats.

Her mouth full, I ask, "Why is Terrell in Taos?"

"A convention," Jordan says, covering her mouth with her hand, "But I was unaware that you were unaware. Earlier, I mean."

"Of what?" I ask, wanting her to say more.

"Of who Terrell is," she says, "Of what he does." She types something into her phone and holds it out to me.

Before I look, I say, "Does he know that you are going to tell me whatever you're going to tell me?"

"He knows you know he's in Taos," Jordan says, shrugging. "I called him before I came over. And he said he *was* in Scotland for a few days, before Taos. He told me that." Terrell's been gone five days. To and from Scotland is a full day of flying. It's *possible* he was in Scotland before returning to the States, to Taos. But, why?

I put on my cheaters and take the phone from Jordan. On the phone is a Wikipedia entry for "Phoenix Lights." I look at Jordan. She is again mid-bite. The entry reads:

The PHOENIX LIGHTS *(also identified as* "LIGHTS OVER PHOENIX"*) was a UFO sighting which occurred in Phoenix, Arizona, and Sonora, Mexico on Thursday, March 13, 1997. Lights of varying descriptions were reported by thousands of people between 19:30 and 22:30 MST, in a space of about 300 miles (480 km), from the Nevada line, through Phoenix, to the edge of Tucson. There were allegedly two distinct events involved in the incident: a triangular formation of lights seen to pass over the state, and a series of stationary lights seen in the Phoenix area. The United States Air Force later identified the second group of lights as flares dropped by A-10 Warthog aircraft that were on training exercises at the Barry Goldwater Range in southwest Arizona.*

I hold out the phone for Jordan who is up and looking for a mug. She's opening cupboards until I point to the right one, and she pours herself coffee. But, I'm not following. I ask her what the deal is, say, here take the phone. She says, "Keep reading." I audibly huff, and she smiles, drinks her coffee. I scroll past sections detailing the timeline of the events, the arrival of the first and second set of lights in Prescott, Dewey, and Phoenix. Scroll past a heading of "First Sighting in Phoenix," and "Reappearance in 2007," and "Reappearance in 2008." I scroll until I reach a section of the entry titled "Photographic Evidence." Details of the photographic evidence of the first event yield nothing of interest; I go to the second event, and jackpot:

During the Phoenix event, numerous still photographs and videotapes were made, distinctly showing a series of lights appearing at a regular interval, remaining illuminated for several moments and then going out. Terrell Presley, of Phoenix, captured the most often reproduced of these images. Presley's photographs were all taken from the upper level of a Phoenix parking garage near Phoenix Sky Harbor International Airport. These images have been repeatedly aired by documentary television channels such as the Discovery Channel and the History Channel as part of their UFO documentary programming. [...] The most frequently reproduced sequence shows what appears to be an arc of lights appearing one by one, then going out one by one. UFO advocates claim that these images show that the lights were some form of "running light" or other aircraft illumination along the leading edge of a large craft—estimated to be as large as a mile (1.6 km) in diameter—hovering over the city of Phoenix. Thousands of witnesses throughout Arizona also reported a silent, mile wide V or boomerang shaped craft with varying numbers of huge orbs. A significant number of witnesses reported that the craft was silently gliding directly overhead at low altitude.

"He's not golfing," I say.

"He golfs. He just also gives talks about the event. He was giving a talk in Taos. There are UFO conventions all over the world. That's where I met Mr. Presley. At a talk he gave in Toronto a year ago."

A year ago. I'm trying to remember where Terrell told me he'd gone, but I couldn't remember. He could've said Canada.

The Phoenix Lights would have happened three months after my wife and I moved to Arizona from Chicago. 1997. Eighteen years ago. I was thirty-seven and she was thirty-nine, no kids, no dog. I was still looking for a new job. I didn't know it at the time, but it would be another two anxious months of unemployment. She was working all sorts of shifts at the hospital, crazy hours, hours she didn't need to work, to prove to her staff she was one of them, and had arrived to stay. They learned quickly the kind of woman she was. I still get cards from these women on her birthday, on my birthday, on days less readily marked. Undoubtedly she was working the night these alien lights hung in the sky. The night Terrell was on the top level of a parking garage taking pictures. Why was he up there? Is the answer because he had the time? I don't know if he'd sold his adhesive patent by then or not. I don't know what his nights were filled with. But, certain types of people don't see UFOs would be my guess, people who are paycheck to paycheck, people with three kids, sick people, people with tangible worries and jobs; this is probably wrong. Maybe witnesses to these events span demographics, maybe because they actually happen.

We had an apartment on the fourth floor and on her days off we'd sit in shorts on our little deck and watch the sunset, ask each other, "Would you move back to Chicago if you could?" And we'd both say, "No, I wouldn't. I like it here." Neither of us believed the other completely. We'd left all our friends, moved to a new state where the people were different, more private, and found we were more unwilling to make new friends than we'd realized. We liked people, both of us, we liked people we didn't know, we liked waiters and pharmacists and kids on airplanes, I mean, we hated all these people too, at times, but I'm just saying we were not wary of everyone unknown to us, we were open, just less open than we'd realized before we'd moved, but we became happier clinging to each other, married in a way we never knew we could be.

I vaguely remember reading about the Phoenix Lights in the paper. Front page news. But, I didn't care about the event. Not in the slightest. I felt this way, feel this way, because of course there are aliens. Even if the lights aren't extraterrestrial, if the reality is that the lights were some military happening, of course there is still something out there. The specifics aren't important to me until the manifestation of alien life appearing on our planet moves past this speculative era. The difference for me is that life is enough. Normal routine nothing is enough. I'm interested in maps and cell phones and recycling. And the rainforest. And ocean fish that pulse glowing at pitch black depths. And baseball. Ford automobiles. Tintypes of my forebears. Helmets from the Han dynasty. The house across the street. My thinking is, aren't we enough? Huddling together in hotel ballrooms and convention centers to affirm the actuality of an event past seems a waste. There's actuality happening right now. In abundance. But, I could be missing the point.

Terrell and I didn't speak until after my wife died. We'd waved to him as we were building this house in Cave Creek, and he'd waved back, but we didn't engage in any conversations in the middle of the street or elsewhere. My wife said at the time that Terrell looked like William Faulkner, then she'd said Howard Hughes, or a short actor playing Howard Hughes in a community theater production.

"A production of what?" I remember asking.

"*Melvin and Howard*," she said, to please me. She knew that the idea of the Demme movie done onstage would make me grin. We'd seen *All the President's Men*, a ten-year anniversary release in '86, on our first date in Rogers Park near the Loyola campus at a theater long since gone, and Robards had remained something like our patron saint ever since. I'd said this to Terrell early on, told him my wife had thought he looked like Faulkner, and he squinted his small eyes, and said he'd never been told that. I think he started telling me about his renters because during that first talk after we were caught checking the mail at the same time, he needed something to say to the widower.

Jordan is washing her own plate and mug, and I'm letting her do so without protest. She's finished, makes eye contact with me, and then looks away, meaning she is going to be heading out. I walk her to the door and she steps outside, turning to me and saying, "When Terrell gets back you should come over for drinks, the three of us." Whatever she knows about Terrell is very different than what I know of him, so, maybe, although I say in my head, "That will never happen," maybe it will. It occurs to me to say, "Today is my Friday, so tomorrow could still work," but then I'd have to explain that for the past several years, since beginning remote consulting, I've reinstated the work schedule of my youth in retail. Friday to Tuesday. It made sense to return to the schedule I knew before married life, to shopping in empty grocery stores midweek. For my life to lack any family rhythm. I say, "Sure, you bet," about potentially drinking together and give her an earnest thumbs-up before she begins back across the street. She's taken four steps, I know because I'm watching her walk away too closely, I'm human, and I say, "Jordan." She stops and faces me. "What's the big fucking secret? Why wouldn't Terrell just tell me where he was going? What he was doing?"

"Maybe he was afraid things would change," she said, "Or maybe he thought you already knew." And I have to remind myself she doesn't know the state of our understanding of one another, how brief and situational our connections are. We speak in the middle of the street about people who will be staying at Terrell's house a handful of times a year. I relay information about past renters. I do not ask Terrell personal questions; I respect the boundaries he maintains through his silence on topics he wishes to avoid. I try to make him laugh, and occasionally get a wry smile, which is just as satisfying. It's possible that Jordan is right about Terrell being adverse to a change in our situation. I can see how if Terrell likes being perceived as a person who keeps up with boyhood pals and takes them golfing around the world (in my previous understanding it was Terrell who paid for dinners and drinks and possibly even hotel rooms for these men) he would not want my perception dashed. Maybe he was able to see himself in the way I saw him because of our talks. Maybe he believes I know of his UFO talks and the golf and can hold those two facts in my head at once without ever speaking of the former. Maybe his understanding was that other people in town had told me of his Phoenix Lights fame and the reason our arrangement worked was because I chose to not ask him of it. Because what was there to say? What is there to say? You believe or you don't, regardless of content. Maybe he knew me to be a believer, in general, and so any talk of inner self-definition and purpose was beside the point. The point was he'd found, in part, an equal. Maybe he wants me to be able to live inside my own created worlds, as I have done for him. I won't be able to ask these questions of Terrell, not in a way that would give me the answers I want to know. And should I ask, I imagine he would raise his eyes to the horizon. I've heard it said colloquially that the ability to communicate is unlimited if a certain openness is allowed by both parties; I believe this to be far from the truth. The amount of self-knowledge pre-supposed in a word like "openness" is inconceivably vast. Our neighborly pattern feels irreparably altered.

Terrell's back. After hearing his garage door motor, I get to the window in time to see him and Jordan pull away in the Saab a few times, and I get no invite for drinks. She leaves sometime after I lose track of their coming and going because an accounting program I helped design for an after-market golf cart accessory manufacturer in the Valley has gone awry. I have to videoconference with the same in-house tech guy for three days straight, giving him the language to calm his three bosses and an understanding of how to fix the books. I tell him at one point when he is losing all patience with the tasks he sees stacked waiting in the days ahead that we are talking about golf cart canopies and GPS systems to determine shot lengths for a leisure sport. This is not life and death. He is not calmed. He tells me this is his job, "It is my job to be worried." I try and let his words stand for him by not responding, in order for him to be able to hear what he's said and re-examine its content. But I don't think this happens. I'm certain it doesn't.

Amvi

This is a story I would never tell my wife. But, when some version of the following does reach Beth, I'll say, "We don't live in Chicago anymore," and hope that fact radiates with meaning, illuminating how much life we've lived since all my most notable mistakes took place, how many consecutive calm years we've had in the interim. I'll tell her, "I can't remember the last time a woman gave me a second look." And every word of that is true. Truest of all: this is a story I would never tell my wife.

East to west the 152 always had flight attendants on it. I'd be on the bus headed to work in the pink morning and see women already in the navy uniform, the scarf and pantyhose, the full makeup, focused, aloof. Conservatively sexualized, with one black rolling carry-on and a purse that could zip shut. There were many of these women, the male variety less common on this bus, and so, not unlike if I was downtown when the ballerinas were released into the city dusk, wearing their civvies on the broad sidewalk near the park: sweats, high cheekbones, pouts, and disinterest; I tried to stay calm.

Off work, west to east on the 152 towards the lake, sun not yet down, I was trying to stay calm, but it was seven o'clock, late July on the north side, I had the next three days off, and no plans. The Cubs were out of town, Cincinnati, meaning there would be less to deal with on the streets. The air was staticky. In the days before it had been storming in the afternoons and middle-night, but on this night it seemed the rain would hold a while longer. And I was trying to stay calm, but she, Amvi, who I did not yet know was Amvi, was reading a book I could speak about, McGuane's *Ninety-Two in the Shade*. Since the time of this story, I've conflated what Amvi looked like with the actress Archie Panjabi, from *The Good Wife*. I believe this conflation is justified. I've tried to blackbox Amvi's face, this story, all particulars, in fear they would appear to me while I slept, and I would unconsciously speak the name "Amvi" aloud in our conjugal bedroom, be forced to sit up and explain myself. Or worse, and more likely, be reminded quietly in the morning and in full daylight, look Beth in the eye and offer some fragment of the truth.

To be clear: saying a name aloud in my sleep and *knowing* my wife will learn some totality of this story are separate fears. The latter, inevitable.

Trying for calm: Amvi, still a stranger, was seated a row ahead at the window, reading. The bus was humid, mostly vacant, its lighting bluish. The seat next to me was empty and the seat next to Amvi was occupied by luggage. I thought she was a flight attendant. Her chaste skirt, collar, the earrings she lacked, that I imagined it was her ritual to remove post-flight. Her copy of the McGuane was paperback, the beautifully spare Penguin edition, with an almost entirely white cover, and a bit of sun and a palm tree in the upper right. Amvi had her hair in two long braids that reached her clavicle.

I leaned forward, "Have you seen the movie?"

"I have no interest," she said, without turning around.

"In movies?" I asked. She smiled.

"McGuane directed it. Warren Oates, Burgess Meredith. It's fun."

"Haven't. I like Warren Oates," she said. *Gallatin Canyon* had been recently published and I told her that it contained what I thought was McGuane's best work. She nodded in a way that gave away nothing. And then our conversation became not so much wish fulfillment for me, but instead, proof that everything is real. That there was a professional woman who could casually talk about *Badlands*, *Two-Lane Blacktop*, Peckinpah, The Penguin and the wonderful black shirts his henchmen wore bearing their names, "Sparrow," and "Hawkeye," and then move through those topics to others, and by "others," I don't mean she spoke about herself. I had to ask to learn anything about Amvi. She told me her father was a film professor in Bloomington, and that her mother was a librarian. That both her parents were from Lucknow, a city that I told her I didn't know. I hadn't yet been to India at the time. Still haven't. I told her everything I knew of India came from Louis Malle. This confused her because she only knew *Murmur of the Heart* and *Alamo Bay*.

"Maybe three million people live there," she said.

She picked up what I now saw was not luggage but a violin case and held it on her lap. I sat down next to her. We spoke our names to each other for the first time and I understood the possibility of seeing her in less of an outfit, in her own apartment. Her apartment, because it would be on her terms. Amvi had been making the rules between us from the first word. From even before then. My place was out of the question.

"You aren't a flight attendant," I said.

"I never said I was," she said. "But I like how often you admit to knowing nothing."

This was before note taking was a task done entirely on phones, and so I had Amvi's address on the back of my brother's business card. At the time he detailed luxury cars in Denver. On the front of the card was a black Ferrari in profile, stripped of all identifiable marking, but unmistakably a Testarossa. Below the car read: "BRAD" and under that "303-766-3902." The back was blank. Amvi's Roscoe Village address was scrawled on the empty side. I had an unopened pack of one hundred of my brother's business cards on an upper shelf in my closet that I'd requested as a birthday gift. The fact that Brad actually gave me such a gift explains my brother well. His name was not always "Brad." He'd renamed himself for what he termed "business purposes," and none of the family was able to prove him wrong because he was making money. Much more than when he'd been Robert. Now that he was steadily earning, the name-change had birthed a mantra he often repeated, "Process is nothing. Work." His revisionist claim was that this mantra had led to the name change and not vice versa. I'd tried to refute his logic and Brad repeated the mantra to me as a counter. I'm not sure he's wrong. And I was standing on the bright street, after ten at night, holding Brad's business card, thinking about nineties sports cars and their relation to the kind of moment I was currently having, looking up at a rugged three-flat where the card told me Amvi lived, when she opened the front door.

She'd changed into a loose, white sleeveless top. Of course, seeing her pull this top over her head and shake her hair out would have been ideal. Her hair was no longer in braids and when I crossed the threshold I could tell she was fresh from the shower. No perfume, just soap and residual warmth emanating. Her lipstick had changed color to red. Amvi put a hand on my chest and asked for collateral.

"Collateral?"

"We're still strangers, aren't we?" she said.

I still didn't know what she meant. I gave her my whole wallet. She looked behind my driver's license, told me she was checking for photographs of other women, saw none, told me "either way would've been fine," and silently tallied the seven ones and single ten dollar bill, and started up the stairs. My phone was vibrating in my pocket and without looking, I ignored the call. I followed her to the second floor watching my wallet in her hand. It's not that I didn't trust Amvi, trust didn't enter my thinking at all. I wasn't thinking. I only wanted to know what was going to happen. How long it would last.

The apartment had a large creaking front room overlooking the street, one bedroom off a long unlit hall, then another bedroom, Amvi's, in the back near the kitchen. The wooden floor was in narrow strips like a worn bowling lane. The place did not feel lived in. There were piles of what appeared to be "work" all over. A thin tabletop with sloughing stacks of papers was at a window facing an alley. Set in front of the street window, a desk chair. Across the street was an antique dealer that Amvi said operated by appointment only. Flanking the antique shop was a dog groomer and an abandoned storefront.

Dark, uniformly renovated apartments above. This front room suggested a stakeout. Amvi said her roommate, who was not home, did pharmaceutical research. I nodded through this explanation of the clutter and reached into my pocket to again decline a call. Her roommate, she told me, was the daughter of a family friend.

"Doesn't that make her a family friend?" I asked.

"It does not," Amvi said.

The apartment's walls were blank except for Amvi's bedroom, of which I was only allowed a glance. She stood in the doorway barring my entrance and simultaneously flipped on the bedroom light. The room was yellow. I saw a huge black and white Willie Nelson poster over her bed, young Willie shirtless and in braids, like Amvi had worn earlier. And there were Chicago Symphony Orchestra posters, small, cheaply framed concert advertisements, maybe five, grouped on the near wall. Amvi tossed my wallet underhand on to her pillow, and led me back to the front, where she carefully lit candles on two windowsills and a coffee table.

"I'd rather have the TV on in the background instead of music if that's OK," she said. She put on a Humphrey Bogart movie that was half over, *Key Largo*. Amvi told me the movie had been on several times recently and she'd read a little about the real island, "Frost has never been recorded on Key Largo." We sat on the couch, me in the middle and Amvi on the far end, her legs tucked underneath her, and I was having trouble understanding what was expected. Again, my phone went off, again, I didn't answer.

"Looks it," I said.

"That's a Warner Brothers backlot," Amvi said.

The formality of being walked around the entire apartment, as if I was a slow-witted relative, coupled with having my wallet stashed on her bed was making me uneasy. My thoughts had stayed in the bedroom, clearly. The wallet signaled a return. Right? She was being playful, yes, but I'd witnessed similar behavior reveal itself to be empty. Bloodless ploys. The candles had given the room the smell of cut grass. Admittedly, I was out of practice.

"You aren't a flight attendant. You *do* play the violin. CSO?"

Amvi smiled and it became obvious to me as she smiled I was in no position to even ask questions. I knew too little. "No," she said. "Viola. I've subbed for the pit orchestra on some of the musicals that run downtown. Twice. I've done that twice. I give lessons—"

My phone buzzed in my pocket. Amvi said, "Pick it up," and gestured with both hands. I stood up and walked into the long hallway that led toward the kitchen and her bedroom.

It was Brad calling. He told me that Beth had called him and didn't care if we were in a fight, didn't care what anyone had said, but to get her phone number blocked was fucked and she would not stand for it. To call the phone company and list her number as one that I would not be receiving calls from, was fucked. Brad said Beth had called him fifteen consecutive times until he answered, and demanded that he call me, and to keep calling until I picked up.

"Fifteen's a real number?"

"After a couple, I wanted to see how long she'd go, but I got scared counting."

"Why didn't she call me from another phone?"

"How would I know that?" Brad asked. "Go home. Deal with your girlfriend. She said you stayed last night at Parker's. Go to Parker's—Parker?—and get your bag, or whatever you took, and go home."

We hung up. I walked into Amvi's bedroom and picked up my wallet from her pillow. I took out my library card and slipped it into her pillowcase. Under her pillow. I frisbeed an expired AAA card into her closet. My thinking wasn't clear. There was no thought. "She started it," was a sentence I had in mind, but this was an isolated imperative with lots of air around it. In the living room I fumbled through an apology to Amvi, told her I had to leave, I'm sorry. I was speaking too loudly. She nodded coolly from the couch, seeming to understand my limitations and impending mawkish return to another woman. When I looked to the second floor windows from the street, the candles were still going. It seemed possible to go back. The rain continued to hold.

To say in my exit I purposely supplied a way for Amvi to potentially show up at our door would be a lie. That I wanted to create some dormant threat. That I'd hoped as we cooked dinner, or came in from a walk with the dog, she'd appear. Calmly at the door. But, when I would picture it, we come in with the dog and Amvi's already in the apartment. She could have started with my name, the knowledge that I lived on the north side, the bus I took home from work, and then maybe convince a Merlo or Sulzer branch employee to match my library card to an address, well, it *is* possible. One can imagine a bribable AAA customer service representative. Beth would remember the fight without much prompting. She would remember how we laughed as I got the woman who worked for Verizon to remove her number from my blocked list. How the woman had told us she handled this exact situation several times a day. How we'd been on speakerphone with the woman together to let her know we'd reconciled. It was important to both of us that she knew we were fine. Blocking a number is easier now. You don't have to call anyone, it's all in the phone.

But I don't believe I was extending an invitation. If anything, I was signaling a return I wasn't capable of making. But not consciously. Like I said, there was no thought. So often in my life, there has been *no* thought. The instinct, because that's what it was, I believe, was to remind myself that the mistake I had made and was making was real. That as unreal as taking the bus to work and glowing skies can seem, as unreal as meeting a woman who can talk about the movies you can talk about can seem, in a different sense than I meant it earlier, everything is real. If the first understanding is something like: everything is possible and already occurring, the second is: I no longer had a library card.

The fragment I'll offer if I have control of the telling is that I met a woman on the bus, we talked on the bus is all, the day after I stayed the night at Parker's all those years ago, when we fought about the plane tickets for your brother's graduation. I'd called your brother a cross-eyed pussy. Of course, we were fighting about lots then. Fighting about fighting. And if in the night I speak Amvi's name I will tell you it was a girl I went to elementary school with. From Peru. And if I have no control over the telling and you hear the whole thing as I am telling it now, I'll say I regret nothing, and am wrong often. And that we don't live in Chicago, and that no woman even notices me anymore. And you'll say you believe me, and that none of that bothers you. And this last part you won't say, but it'll be a look you give me, because you understand where my thoughts have been and for how long, and why. And your look will explain my fear, my guilt, your look will say, "She's still here."

Acknowledgments

Thank you to Maxx Loup and Drew Marquart for being willing readers over the years; I'm lucky. To friends in Chicago and elsewhere—your encouragement was invaluable. Thank you to Jeff Blair. Thank you to Judd Mealey. Thank you to Shane Jones, Stuart Dybek, Christine Sneed, Naeem Murr, Shauna Seliy, and Brad Watson. Thank you to everyone at Tailwinds Press. Thank you to my family. And thank you Brittany and Mo for the love and tolerance.

Credits

Some of these stories appeared in the following journals, sometimes in a slightly different form:

"Surfers"- *Dark Fucking Wizard*
"No Door"- *Dark Fucking Wizard*
"Wolf is a River in Germany"- *Fanzine*
"Warning" - *Paper Darts*
"Banking"- *New World Writing*
"Cardinal"- *PANK*
"One Dead, Sets Fire"- *The Adroit Journal*
"Shelly"- *The Adroit Journal*
"A Father's Story"- *Burrow Press Review*
"How I Got This Job"- *Dark Fucking Wizard*
"Loose Routine"- *DOGZPLOT*
"On a Warm Night"- *Hobart*

A information can be obtained
.ICGtesting.com
in the USA
2s0336140917
0LV00003B/218/P

9 780996 717526

About the Author

ALEX HIGLEY lives in Chicago with his wife and dog. He is working on a novel.

CPSI
at www
Printed
LVOW
54870